LUNA STATION
QUARTERLY

Issue 056 | December 2023

The Horse Issue

Editor-in-Chief

Jennifer Lyn Parsons

Editors

Katrina Carruth • Sara Doan • Carly Racklin • Shana Ross
Katrina Schroeder • Gô Shoemake • Bridget Siniakov • Izzy Varju
Loretta M Haskell • Sarah McPherson • Caite Sajwaj
Sophia Thimmes • Jamie M. Boyd • Maria Brekke • Rine Karr

LUNA STATION PRESS
NEW JERSEY

First Paperback Edition December 2023
ISBN: 978-1-949077-46-9

Luna Station Quarterly publishes short fiction on March 1st, June 1st,
September 1st, and December 1st. For more information and submission
guidelines, please visit our website at lunastationquarterly.com

For Luna Station Press

Creative Director—Tara Quinn Lindsey

Editor-in-Chief & Founder—Jennifer Lyn Parsons

LUNA STATION PRESS

www.lunastationpress.com

CONTENTS

Editorial

Jennifer Lyn Parsons

Jennifer Lyn Parsons is a writer and senior software engineer. Currently, she enjoys writing fantasy stories about middle-aged people who aren't into the whole "going on a quest" thing but do it anyway. When not writing code or prose, she is also the editor-in-chief of the venerable Luna Station Quarterly. She finds joy in baseball, tea, discovering music new and old, and making analog things.

Horses loom large in our collective histories. Symbols of power, of strength, companions on a long journey, heroes, magical creatures, etc. they're woven through the fabric of our tales.

I don't recall when I started loving them, though for most of my life I had no contact with them whatsoever. There would be an occasional pony ride at the school fair or a petting zoo would give me the opportunity to interact with them, and despite my limited experience with the real, live creatures, they occupied an outsized portion of my mind and day dreams.

My grandmother took me to see "The Last Unicorn" in 1982. It was a big deal because my little brother was not with us, nor the rest of my family. It was just me and Grandma at the movies together. It felt very grown up somehow. I was only seven at the time and watching the film more recently, I'm impressed with my young self for being so brave. There were some scary moments!

Of course I really wanted the titular Unicorn of the film to be my friend. She was so pretty and magical. She was my first real exposure to unicorns and I always find it interesting that I don't really have a memory of anyone telling me what a unicorn was, I just accepted that she was one. I guess it goes along somewhere with someone telling you what a whale is, or a cat, or a more down-to-earth horse. They appear and, like magic, you know what they are and don't question it.

I'm honestly not sure what it is about horses that romances me so. All I know is that my few opportunities to go on a trail ride have only solidified that love. Up close horses have a big energy and I've often longed to stay with whatever trail horse deigns to carry me and become better friends. They can be patient if you're lucky or persnickety if you're not, and they have a smell to them that I'm glad to carry with me for the rest of the day.

Alas, owning a horse is not in the cards for me right now. Instead, my childhood collection of books on horse breeds and horse care still sit on the bookshelf behind me as I write this. I spent hours and hours pouring over them, learning how to clean out a hoof, properly adjust a saddle, and a million other skills I would never get to put to use. I probably spent even more time admiring the different breeds and drawing my own copies of the pictures in my books.

All this love of horses is pouring out here and now, the obvious inspiration for this year's theme. There's such a wild and varied selection of stories in this issue, tales full of magic and mayhem, court intrigues and cybernetic mounts. And of course, a few unicorns for good measure. It's nothing less than you might expect from a stories centered on a creature with such presence in the tales we've told around a fire for millennia. I hope you enjoy the ride.

L S Q | 056

walking slowly
favorite field
evening rounds

the horse looks up
remembering the
day they came

and changed everything

the horse has no one
to ask about this memory
of friendship and flight

of strange food and strange
stars and stories that can
never be shared with

anyone who walks the earth

so the horse bears
the mystery with
grace, loving

the scent of the grass
as the sun sets and
the laughter of

friends rings over the hill

words by Quinn - 11.19.23

Misty Moon

Elizabeth Hinckley

As a naturalist and an author, Elizabeth Hinckley has a passion for both the natural world and the power of story, and their ability to inspire the human spirit. She is the author of David, A Rat. She lives in New Jersey, home to a surprisingly beautiful and diverse array of natural wonders, which she explores frequently.

Claire could not believe what she was seeing as she stared into the unexpectedly empty space. As she worked her way down each stall in the horse barn, doling out dinner and hay flakes, each of the horses had been agitated, pacing and ignoring their food. She knew to listen to her animals, understanding that bad weather rolling in or the scent of some nearby predator could get them all spooky, but the weather was fine and in fact, the sun was gearing up for a spectacular sunset. The livestock dogs had not alerted to any coyotes or anything. They were, in fact, lying in the barnyard quietly, facing the sunset as if enjoying a day at the beach. The absence of any obvious trouble made the horses' agitation even more unnerving.

The unease followed her as she did her work, the reason only making itself known when she reached Misty's stall and found it empty. She stood there staring for a minute. The dust motes swirling around in the afternoon light matched her thoughts, slowly floating around back in on themselves, because it frankly made no sense. Misty was her own pet horse and there was no reason anyone else in the family would have taken her out. Life on a ranch had its surprises, but was orderly and regimented so that everything got done properly every day. There were no farrier or vet visits, it was late in the day, a time when all the horses would be in anyway, and the rest of the family had gone up to town—there was no reason for her to be gone. Even so, she turned her head to look down the aisle, and spotted the horse trailer parked across the yard, confirming that Misty hadn't been taken anywhere.

Confounded, she entered the stall to look over the door into the turn-out yard—it wouldn't make sense for Misty to still be out, since Claire had just brought her inside a half hour ago before going to prepare the feed buckets. Granted, she had turned up the dusty old boombox in order to sing along because no one else was around; it would have been too embarrassing to do so if anyone within a five mile radius was around to hear her belting out that the "best thing about being a woman is the prerogative to have a little fun" as she dumped horse feed with flair from a scoop held high above her head into the bucket. It was the only reason she wouldn't have heard something going on in the barn, and probably the reason it took her a few minutes longer than usual, too.

As expected, she didn't see Misty in her fenced-in turn out yard either, but as she put her hand on the half door, it opened outwards into the yard. Looking down to examine it, she saw that the strong iron latch—whose very purpose was to be secure and horse proof—had been ripped from the wood by the screws, which now dangled from the door. The door itself was intact, but bore crescent-shaped dents in the wood: hoof prints from a gentle horse that never acted up.

Misty was a quiet little Quarter Horse whose usual track from the barn to the yard led to a muddy patch on the side fence, a favorite area for keeping an eye on barnyard activities, and from which she could spot her human pal when she came out of the house. Likewise, there was a little trail in the grass from the back door to that spot, showing that Claire's usual path went from the back door to Misty's spot before going anywhere else. She had once been a working horse, but was cow-hocked in her rear legs. It hadn't caused her any soundness problems yet, but she was a little under-horsepowered because of it, and had been retired a few years ago to leisurely riding and companionship to a younger Claire, who had waited patiently for her very own horse. It took her another few minutes to even consider that Misty had jumped the fence—something she had never done, and which Claire even doubted she could do.

But at the end of the turnout yard, the soil was all torn up, as if Misty had been running the fence line back and forth. Walking the outside of the fence, Claire found hoof prints sunk deep into the soil on the far side, and a track pattern spread out by several feet that clearly indicated Misty had taken off at a gallop.

"Goddamn it, Misty." Claire muttered to herself. It was not said in anger, but worry. The sun would be down soon, and the ranch opened out onto miles of BLM lands—huge tracts of public land. Since there was no obvious reason for her to have run off, there was no telling where she had gone, or how far. She might very well come home on her own, but this whole thing was highly unusual, and she was afraid for Misty. There is nothing so isolated as a herd animal alone, and breaking a leg in a gopher hole or getting attacked by predators were real dangers, so Claire wanted to find her as soon as possible. Mom would not be happy with her going out by herself, but the family was at her little brother's big game tonight, and he was so excited for it. She wasn't going to ruin the evening, or waste time, by going up to town to fetch them.

Running back to the house, the livestock dogs perked up their heads. "Good work, boys. You really kept an eye on things," she grumbled at them sarcastically. Unconcerned, or perhaps embarrassed, they turned back to watching the sunset. She didn't have time to think about how strange it was for them to have let this happen. They were usually very good working dogs, always on top of things.

There was no time to leave a detailed note, so she picked up the phone and called her best friend Megan, laying out the details of her planned search area. She hoped to get back before her family got home sometime around 10, but if not, Megan would call the house and let them know where to go look for her. Then she got on the ATV and took off in the direction of the hoof prints.

***

Despite the urgency of the current situation, Claire felt capable and prepared riding out into the rangelands. She had a gun just in case, but she wasn't afraid of coyotes unless there was a large pack, and with the heat of the day gone, the snakes would be going to ground for the night. It was pretty remote, so it was unlikely she would stumble on any people, but for that reason, any she stumbled on would really be up to no good: drug-deals-and-body-dumping no good. She'd watch for dust clouds now and headlights later as the sun set to avoid anybody like that.

For a while, she followed hoof prints where she could find them, but at some point, they gave out where the ground became too hard to show them. She noted the spot and designated it as Misty's last known location, then imagined search trajectories from there. She tried two of them before returning to the spot, covering miles. The sun was going down, but it was a full moon tonight, so she would still be able to see—at least until her turnaround time. Looking at her fanned out trajectories, which she had divided into 5 pie slices from the the last known location, she realized she only had time for one more. She had done the leftmost and center slices, but just outside the zone of the rightmost pie slice, backtracking a bit, there was a hill. With only one shot left in daylight, she changed tactics and headed for it, hoping to get a view.

Near the bottom of the hill, she crossed churned up ground. "Mustangs!" she realized with dismay. They hadn't wandered this close to the ranch in years. "Oh girl..." Claire thought with dismay. "Now you've gone and run away from home... or you're coming home knocked up." A little mustang baby out of Misty would probably be adorable, but Mom and Dad would not be pleased with another non-working mouth to feed. But that was a problem, granted a big problem, that didn't compare to the present one of actually getting her back at all.

Claire refocused her mind to the task. Following the trampled ground, the tracks led right to a small river—and ended. Judging from the muddy riverbank full of holes, the herd had clearly crossed it, but it was too deep for wading, or for the ATV. Out of time and daylight, she cursed and stomped with frustration, knowing that this was the practical end of the search for the night. She would have to return with help in the daytime.

For now, there was one last thing: she could ride the ATV up the hill, and maybe see if the herd had left a dark track across the wide open grassland. Turning away from the river, she circled to the back side of the hill where the slope was more gradual. She rode to the crest and turned off the motor in order to hear better. The sun had now set, but there was still a rosy glow in the western sky, and the full moon had cleared the eastern horizon. In every direction, the sky seemed infinite, pricked with stars in a sky pale blue enough to seem like some alternate version of daylight, the details of the land below clear and visible. Then Claire felt the strange sensation of unease she had felt in the barn. It was not fear, so much as the sense that something was "off"—that something was out of the ordinary, but not in a way she could articulate. And in that moment, she looked just past where the curve of the river hugged the hill, and saw a large herd of wild mustangs gathered.

They didn't seem to notice her. The wind blew from their direction, taking her scent far away from them. Coming up the opposite side of the hill and then cutting the engine, the noise from the ATV must have been carried off by the wind. But if she could have flown in a straight line from the top of the hill to the center of the herd, it couldn't have been more than 200 feet.

More astonishingly, the herd was behaving strangely. The loose group of horses started to spread out, like grease with a drop of dish soap in it. They formed a circle, perfectly shaped, with each horse facing in towards a completely cleared center. And in that center stood a beautiful pinto mustang.

It had a coat of gleaming chestnut patches on white, with streaks of both colors in its mane and tail—gleaming, because just then, the moon crested the hill and shone right on the circle of the herd, setting their forms alight and giving Claire goosebumps. But most striking was its entirely white head. She knew horses, and had seen every variation of color: pintos with all of their various colored patches, horses with blazes and stars on their faces, Appaloosas with their spotted rumps, horses named One Sock, Two Socks, plain old Socks, and Boots; piebalds, paints, and 'paperfaced' horses with all white faces and blue eyes. There were even some with white faces and dark ears, called 'medicine hat' horses—but never in her life had she seen, or even heard of, a horse with an all white head—even ears and forelock. The coloring didn't even seem genetically possible as far as she knew. The curve of the white cheek made a distinctive line against the neck, where the chestnut patches started. It was as if someone had placed the head of a white horse on some other horse.

The horse's face captured the moonlight so that the horse seemed to glow. All of the other horses stood quietly facing in, as if in some sort of communion. No tails swished, no hooves shifted. They stood there as the moon shadows shifted around them, and Claire was mesmerized. Finally, the horse lifted its head, looking straight at her. She felt like she had been hit by a wave or perhaps a blast of cool wind, yet nothing moved, and all of the horses stood still. At first, she almost felt ashamed for seeing something that seemed secret, but realized there was no reproach in the horse's eyes. Somehow, there was something in this horse's eyes so important it couldn't be contained. It was a feeling as heavy as a fist-sized diamond, and just as complex—facets upon facets of feeling. She'd never be able to explain it, or hold onto it, but she would never be the same again. As strongly as anything she ever knew, she knew this.

The horse finally broke the gaze, and gave a soft nicker. To her astonishment, Claire watched every single horse turn to the left, and start moving. Like any group of living things, or even cars at a traffic light, there is always a little lag between when the first one starts moving followed by each one in turn. But somehow, like a choreographed dance, each horse turned at the same moment, took a few steps, and broke into a gallop, encircling the horse. The speed increased and the circle widened. Covered by the pounding sound of thunderous hoofbeats, Claire threw herself running down the hill to get closer. Hidden in the shrubs by the river, she stared at the mass of horses racing, racing around—and in that maelstrom, she caught a glimpse of a chestnut horse wearing a hot pink halter, appearing predictably every few moments as the mass swirled like a wild carousel. Misty. Her own little hay sucker, usually content to follow the routines of the barn and do as she was asked—blazing around in an electrifying circuit— something entirely primal and beautiful.

A shrill neigh rang out, and all of the horses screeched to a stop, leaning back into their rear legs, some hopping about and all worked up. Then, the white headed horse moved through the perimeter, and like a shot, he led the entire herd galloping away.

Claire watched them go, feeling astonished and unable to move. There was no question now about catching Misty tonight, but Claire felt no worry for her—she seemed in good company. Finally checking her watch, the spell broke as she realized there was no time to waste; she had better beat her folks home before they activated a search.

The open land stretched out before her, and the ATV rolled her placidly towards home under an infinite sky as thoughts of the herd and its mysterious leader quietly swirled insider her head. She pulled in just as the lights of the family pickup rolled up the long drive, and told them the story of the evening, but only that she had spotted Misty with a herd of mustangs—not what they had done. Mom was indeed not happy that she had gone out by herself, but Dad understood. Both were sympathetic and promised to help look for her in the morning.

Setting the alarm for just before dawn, Claire laid her head down and slept peacefully. She awoke early ready for the search, but as soon as she went to the barn for equipment, there was Misty in the barn aisle, outside of her stall door, waiting for someone to open it and give her breakfast.

Claire approached her with quiet relief, and they rested foreheads against each other, breathing each other's breath in the glow of the sun's first rays. Although Claire was always caring, always loving, she had seen herself as being in gentle authority over Misty—a maternalism that expressed itself in responsibility and leadership. But seeing her last night, Claire realized that it was only her own childish sense of self-importance, and that Misty had her own life and experiences outside of Claire's orbit. Like a good mother,

Misty was the one who had let her child feel proud of her developing confidence and accomplishments, allowing her to believe they were wholly her own. As they breathed together, this understanding rooted itself in Claire's heart. With each breath, the roles blurred between them from mother to daughter, daughter to mother, friend to friend...all just translations for love.

As the sun rose higher, morning sounds started coming from the house—the kitchen window sliding up, the door to the equipment barn being opened. Soon, they would come out ready to search, and Claire figured she shouldn't keep them in suspense. Pulling away, she looked Misty over—she seemed tired and dirty, but fine. The secret of the night before seemed to fade, the way mist on a lake gives way before the heat of the sun.

Claire tenderly picked a burr from Misty's forelock, but as she brushed the hair to the side, something strange caught her eye—something that made her stomach drop at the terrible thought that maybe this was some other horse. Checking carefully, she took in the pink halter, the cow-hocked back legs, the little scar on the horse's right front breast. As if showing up to her stall and greeting Claire the way she had wasn't enough, Misty leaned over and nuzzled her shoulder in the very particular way she always did, confirming without a doubt, that it was indeed her. Claire brushed away the moment of madness and leaned into the beloved head, the comforting warmth and smell of her that felt like home.

"I don't have a good explanation for this one," she said thoughtfully, staring at the spot where Misty had always sported a tiny white star on her pretty face. "But, what I do think...maybe we'll keep it between us." Sometime in the past mysterious night, the star had expanded outward, to form a perfectly round circle. Like the full moon.

Horse Girls Til The End

SK Marre

SK Marre is a Connecticut based author and photographer. When she isn't writing magazine articles about the best shutter speeds to capture a sunset, she's probably mountain biking, being bossed around by the cat (the dog has better manners), or working on her fiction. SK has short stories and flash fiction in the Northern Connecticut Writers Workshop: Anthology 2020, Havok Publishing (previously Havok Magazine), Unfortunately, Literary Magazine and History Through Fiction. You can find SK on twitter @SkMarre, instagram @skmarre_author, or through her website, http://www.skmarre.com/.

August 9, 2023

4:27pm

Molly

@amelie what was that company you
used to trailer those mules?

Amelie

Thistle Ridge equine transport. Why?

MC LIKED A MESSAGE

6:05pm

Molly

@everyone who do y'all use for an
emergency vet these days?

Heather

Dog vet?

Molly

Sorry, horse. I guess our last guy retired.

Regina

Yeah, he moved to Florida a few years ago.

Try Dr. Weber over at Pine Brook. If she's not on call, Dr. McDonald is good.

*MacDonald. Stupid autocorrect.

Amelie

If they're not on call, I like Dr. Bruce at Unicorn Veterinary Practice.

I think his real name is Dr. Roberts or something, but everyone calls him Bruce.

Also, why do you need a vet? :suspicioussquint:

Heather

haha your new vet office is called Unicorn? Massachusetts is weird.

RF LAUGHED AT A MESSAGE

AS LAUGHED AT A MESSAGE

Molly

Thanks guys!

August 10, 2023

8:55am

MC REPLIED TO A MESSAGE - "ALSO, WHY DO YOU
NEED A VET? :SUSPICIOUSSQUINT:"

Found a Clydesdale in bad shape. Owner died
and I guess no one realized at first? Horse is a
rack of bones. Huge wound on his side. Brought
him back to my place last night. Took today
and tomorrow off so I can get him settled.

Regina

Oh damn. Was Dr. Weber on call and willing to
drive that far? You're in the middle of nowhere.

Molly

The Rhode Island border is not the middle of nowhere.
I'm literally an hour from your house, Reggie. Lol

And yeah, thankfully. The bastard demon-horse kept
trying to bite us. He lunged at Weber's face, the
ungrateful prick. But I think he's just
lashing out from fear or pain?

Regina

Be careful around him, Mol. A mean horse is
dangerous. A mean horse his size can be deadly.

Molly

Yeah, yeah, I remember our motto. 'You can
love them, but never fully trust them.' lol

Regina

It's a good rule.

Molly

Anyway, Weber sedated him and cut away the
necrotic tissue around his ribs. :pukeface:

It's stitched up with a drain and bandaged now...
obviously he'll be on stall rest for a while.

Regina

Was it as bad as that other horse we rescued? With
the leg wound? What the hell was her name?

Molly

That chestnut with the mile long back. Uh...Julie?
No, Sweet Pea! And yeah. A lot more maggots in this
one. I honestly don't know how he's still alive. I'm
pretty sure most horses wouldn't have survived.

Regina

He's special.

Amelie

A rescue horse! God, it's been years.
Glad you're back at it, though.

Horse girls til the end! :cowgirlface:

Also, he sounds spiteful, not special.

Heather

Like you? Lol

Amelie

Maybe. I plan to live forever, too.

Heather

Did it stink?

Molly

The wound? Of course.

Heather

The dead guy.

Molly

Dead woman, actually. They found her in the woods behind her house, face down in a creek.

Regina

Really? That's sad.

MC LIKED A MESSAGE

Heather

What the hell was she doing out there? :confusedface:

Amelie

Wait, I thought what's his face was allergic to horses/not being an asshole?

HB LAUGHED AT A MESSAGE

Regina

@amelie ! :shockedface:

Molly

I kicked Larry out last week after we got home.

Regina

You did? Are you okay?

Molly

Sort've? We talked about a ring and marriage. I
figured the Scotland trip was where he'd ask.

Amelie

cough You don't need a marriage to be
happy. *cough* Especially not to some biker-
gang-wanna-be-piece-of-trash. *cough*

Molly

We went to see the giant horse head statues on our
last day. I forgot their name, but they're super cool.
Before we left I hinted at a proposal. Like, we were
running out of time, right? Larry just laughed at me.

Heather

I'm sorry, Mol. That sucks.

Regina

Air hugs.

Molly

Ame's right. I don't need a ring. But I'm not gonna
waste more years with someone who won't take
a future with me seriously, married or not.

RF LOVED A MESSAGE

HB LOVED A MESSAGE

AS LOVED A MESSAGE

Regina

How did he take the break up?

Molly

Not well. He said some...things.

Amelie

See asshole note above. He's always been controlling. Mol breaking up with HIM instead of the other way around? I bet he blew up.

Regina

@amelie ! :angryface:

What kind of things, @molly ?

Molly

Oh, you know. The usual. You'll regret this. Watch your back. Same things he always says when he's mad. It'll blow over, though. It always does.

Amelie

Having it blow over doesn't mean you should take him back, though.

Molly

I won't. Not this time.

RF LIKED A MESSAGE

HB LIKED A MESSAGE

AS LOVED A MESSAGE

Molly

So anyway, now I've got time to fill and
horses are better than crying.

Amelie

Horses are monsters but not the
kind that break hearts. Lol

Heather

Well, *yours* are monsters.

Amelie

Just the pony.

Regina

You spelled 'thoroughbred' wrong.

MC LAUGHED AT A MESSAGE

HB LAUGHED AT A MESSAGE

Amelie

Gasp! My turdybred is perfect.

Molly

Figure I can focus on this rescue horse for now. Maybe
I'll feel better after I find him a forever home.

Amelie

You should also find a good looking cowboy
to help around the farm. Shirtlessness
helps a girl heal. It's science.

Molly

Gtg. Farrier is here.

10:27am

Molly

I swear to God, the set of shoes on Clyde
(better name suggestions welcome) were made
of lead. They've got to weigh 20lbs each.

Heather

How were his feet?

Molly

Too long. No laminitis, though, which is a miracle. Like

seriously. Somehow he's survived a septic gash AND isn't limping after all this neglect? It's really amazing.

Amelie

Like I said. The magic of spitefulness.

MC LAUGHED AT A MESSAGE

Molly

Farrier cut back what he could but scheduled another trim in three-ish weeks. Wanted to give the tendons time to stretch.

Or unstretch?

Whatever.

Heather

How long since the last trim?

Molly

Farrier and vet both guessed six months. Between that and how skinny he is...well, the lady must have been sick for a while and not able to care for him. I'm surprised his shoes didn't rip off on their own.

Amelie

SPITE

Heather

Did you give him anything for the pain?

Molly

Clyde? Or the farrier? Haha

Heather

Uh oh. Was Clyde bad?

Molly

Only a little. Just one freakout. Tiny, really.

Heather

Was that in sarcasm font?

10:39am

Molly

@everyone Farrier says hiiiiiii. Also, 'for a good nail' is just as funny as a Venmo memo as it used to be on his check memo.

HB LAUGHED AT A MESSAGE

Regina

Good thing his wife likes us. Lol

12:30pm

Amelie

Dodger?

Molly

??

Amelie

Name suggestion...because he's a draft horse.

Molly

Draft dodger? *:rollingeyes:*

The 60's called. They want their joke back.

HB LIKED A MESSAGE

August 11, 2023

6:14pm

Molly

@heather, Reggie and Ame are stopping by to see
Dodger tomorrow. You working? Want to come? It's
supposed to thunderstorm but maybe y'all can carpool?

Heather

I'm at the hospital all day. *:sadface:*

August 12, 2023

1:35pm

Amelie

@heather this wound definitely smells like a rot.

Heather

Is Dodger being a good boy today?

Molly

He just tried to bite Amelie. Haha

More like a nibble, I guess. And he's giving her the cranky ears.

Amelie

He's giving everyone the cranky ears!

@heather He's mostly just got a bad attitude. He's not actually attacking me. Hard to say how he'll be after he heals up and puts on weight, though. Remember Granny? She was a rack of bones, too. Nice until she wasn't.

Heather

Aww, I liked Granny.

Amelie

Because she didn't pin you in the
corner and try to kill you. :horse:

:dagger:

RF LAUGHED AT A MESSAGE

Regina

@heather, don't listen to them. Dodger hasn't really
lashed out since Dr. Weber stitched him up, so I blame
the maggots. He won't be another Granny. Besides,
I can tell Mol already loves him and his spicy-tude.

Molly

Pffft. He won't be a foster fail, I swear it!

RF LAUGHED AT A MESSAGE

Molly

@heather, he's going through, like, thirty-
five gallons of water a day.

Heather

That seems excessive.

Molly

You still have those extra buckets in your garage?
Or did you sell them with the farm? Weber
said stall rest & hand walking for probably five
weeks. I've only got the two buckets and would
rather not be filling them every few minutes.

Heather

I've got them. I can meet up tomorrow night.

MC LIKED A MESSAGE

Heather

First rule of owning horses

more buckets.

Regina

@heather, hahaha Mol just said 'not owning,
damnit. Especially now that I remember
how much work it takes' hahaha

We'll see about that!

August 13, 2023

6:32am

Molly

Guys. His name is actually Clyde. I got a voicemail from the dead lady's kid saying they found his bridle and want me to take it. Their mom was real weird about it, I guess. Kept it in a locked box labeled 'Clyde'.

MC FORWARDED 4-56421354-5545.MP4

Amelie

Dodger is a better name.

9:45am

Molly

Can confirm, dead lady was weird. I pulled the bridle from its lockbox and there was a note underneath. It just said, 'No.'

Heather

Uhhhh... :suspicioussquint:

RF LIKED A MESSAGE

AS LIKED A MESSAGE

Molly

There was also a book about mythological creatures.

Amelie

Like my unicorn vet?

MC LAUGHED AT A MESSAGE

Molly

Water ones. Like mermaids and kraken.

Heather

Did I mention *:suspicioussquint:*

Regina

Yup. Weird.

10:01pm

Molly

The Greeks were VERY preoccupied with drowning. The sirens, the hydra, the scylla...

Heather

You're actually reading that book?

Molly

Lots of free time, remember? :shrug:

Amelie

You're back to the office tomorrow, no?
Hopefully that'll distract you.

RF LIKED A MESSAGE

August 14, 2023

7:14am

Molly

Clyde-Dodger says thank you for the
extra buckets @heather !

Amelie

His name is Dodger!

Molly

Also, I'm gonna need to get more betadine and gauze
pads. But the gash doesn't look as swollen, so that's good.

MC FORWARDED A56GH781.JPG

45

Molly

There is a whole chapter about equines in this book. Y'all ever heard of a nuckelavee?

Regina

Nucka-what?

Molly

Skinless man riding a skinless horse-demon. Orcadian folklore.

Amelie

Larry?

Molly

??

Amelie

I thought you said spineless.

AS LAUGHED AT A MESSAGE

Molly

Did you just laugh at your own joke?

Regina

Speaking of Larry, how are you doing, Mol?

Molly

Meh.

Regina

Want to talk about it?

Molly

About trying to process the trauma from a
manipulative, controlling ex? Meh.

Regina

We're here for you when you're ready. Air hugs.

MC LOVED A MESSAGE

11:27pm

Molly

Wine. It is good.

August 17, 2023

5:55am

Molly

Ugh. Never drinking again.

August 18, 2023

6:42am

Regina

@molly How's Dodger doing?

(And how are you doing?)

7:36am

Amelie

I think the wine got her.

Regina

I hope not... *:frownface:*

August 20, 2023

7:10am

Molly

Nurse @heather ! *HORSE RELATED QUESTION, I SWEAR* How long for people-lacerations to heal?

Amelie

When you say it like that.... :suspicioussquint:

Heather

Depends. Six to eight weeks if they're deep. More if they're life threatening. Less if they're shallow.

Molly

Huh.

Heather

Why?

Molly

I'm pretty sure the vet said five weeks, but this looks like it'll be healed up way sooner.

MC FORWARDED A56GH793.JPG

Heather

Must have been shallower than it seemed? :shrug:

Molly

Yeah. I guess.

MC FORWARDED A56GH794.JPG

MC FORWARDED A56GH795.JPG

Amelie

From that last picture angle, the wound
looks almost completely closed.

Molly

I think I'll turn him loose in the round
pen. Just for a few minutes.

8:01am

Molly

Fingers x'd he doesn't re-tear anything!

MC FORWARDED A56GH796.JPG

RF LOVED A MESSAGE

HB LOVED A MESSAGE

Regina

> He looks so happy! His ears aren't
> even cranky! :hearteyes:

8:27am

Molly

> Stupid freaking horse. I went to clean his stall, and
> the bastard smashed the gate open. I ran out but he'd
> already taken off. Got all the way to the neighbor's
> cow-fence. Found him screaming, pacing, and pawing.

Amelie

> The electric stopped him?

Molly

> Yeah. :angryface:

> The river's swollen with all the rain, so the neighbor's
> bull is grazing closer to my property than normal.
> Thankfully he didn't react and the herd didn't stampede.

Amelie

> Dodger's okay? Not bleeding or limping?

Molly

> He's fine.

Amelie

> I can come help you string some wire on Dodger's paddock tonight, if you want? I have an old solar charger we can hook up to keep it zappy.

Molly

> Yes please.

9:45am

Amelie

> Oh good, it's raining. Again. Should be fun putting up a fence in this. lol

Molly

> Hopefully it stops before tonight.

6:07pm

Molly

> On the record, I owe Ame a beer and cookies. Behold, a zappy fence! Take that, Dodger!

MC FORWARDED A56GH799.JPG

RF LIKED A MESSAGE

HB LIKED A MESSAGE

10:56pm

Molly

@everyone DUDES! Pretty sure the dead lady thought Dodger was a kelpie. (Like the Scottish horse statues! I finally remembered their name!) She had this whole section highlighted, with exclamation points and underlines.

HB LAUGHED AT A MESSAGE

Molly

Kelpies haunt rivers and streams, usually in the shape of a horse. The kelpie will drag riders into the river and then kill them. Kelpies can summon floods to drown people. A kelpie's tail entering the water sounds like thunder. And if you pass a river and hear wailing or howling, it could be a kelpie warning of an approaching storm.

Heather

She really was weird. Haha

Molly

A kelpie's weak spot is its bridle. Anyone who holds a kelpie's bridle will control it. The MacGregor clan has a kelpie's bridle. It's said to have come from an ancestor who took it from a kelpie near Loch Slochd.

Regina

Was the dead lady Scottish?

Amelie

What does that even mean? 'Hold' his bridle? Like in your hands?

Molly

Maybe? And maybe?

Amelie

Let me look it up.

Wikipedia makes it seem like you have to 'possess' the bridle. As in take it off the kelpie. If you give it back to the kelpie, you no longer control it.

Molly

No longer control it? Meaning you no longer control the bridle? Or the kelpie?

Amelie

Yes? To both?

Regina

Wait, didn't you say the shoes were lead? Isn't that a magic thing?

Nope. I checked. Iron is the metal that kills fairies.

Molly

Is iron heavy? The shoes were stupid heavy.

Farrier didn't say anything about them being weird so maybe they were just normal draft horse shoes?

AS REPLIED TO A MESSAGE "IS IRON HEAVY? THE SHOES WERE STUPID HEAVY."

Then they definitely weren't aluminum. That's super light. The turdybred wears them.

Heather

Ame, Reggie, Mol, you know this kelpie stuff is nonsense, right? RIGHT?? :suspicioussquint:

August 21, 2023

6:52am

Regina

Dodger screamed at the neighbor's river, then it rained. :rofl:

Just saying.

HB LAUGHED AT A MESSAGE

Heather

Okay. :rollingeyes:

August 22, 2023

11:53am

Molly

Larry called me today.

Regina

How'd that go?

Molly

I didn't pick up. He keeps leaving voicemails and I keep deleting them.

Actually, I started listening to one but he just screamed for, like, a minute straight. Then I deleted it half-listened to. I also sent him a text telling him to stop harassing me.

Regina

Good! I know it's hard, but you're moving forward. That's what's gonna heal you.

Molly

I don't need a crappy man. I've got a crappy horse. Lol

Regina

Did Dodger break anything else?

Molly

Nah. He's actually been really good. Sweet
as pie. Kinda weird how quickly his attitude
turned around, but I'll take it!

RF LOVED A MESSAGE

Regina

I knew it! You're falling in love!

Molly

Maybe. Lol But still, don't let me foster fail him.
I also love having money and free time.

RF LAUGHED AT A MESSAGE

August 25, 2023

3:34pm

Molly

Vet pulled the drain out of Dodger's side.
He was a perfect gentleman. Gave me
kisses and snuffles the whole time.

Amelie

Weber sedated him, right?

Molly

Yeah. lol

Amelie

So of course he was good.

Molly

Didn't your thoroughbred flip/break the crossties after she'd already been sedated?

Amelie

We're not talking about her. We're talking about Dodger. :haloemoji:

MC LAUGHED AT A MESSAGE

Molly

Vet was surprised at how quickly Dodger healed up. Said another few days to let the drain holes heal and I should be able to lunge him.

AS LOVED A MESSAGE

RF LOVED A MESSAGE

HB LOVED A MESSAGE

August 26, 2023

9:34am

Molly

@everyone !!! Dodger broke out of his stall. Figured out how to unclip the door latch, that jerk. I walk in carrying his bridle so I can hang it in the tack room, and watch him fling the door open. Then he starts trotting down the aisle.

Amelie

Of course he does.

Molly

So I yell whoa.

Amelie

Did he ignore you, because he's a big dumb draft (dodging) horse?

HB LAUGHED AT A MESSAGE

Molly

He froze on the spot. Like FROZE. Immediately.

Heather

What a good boy.

10:04am

Regina

The bridle controls the kelpie!

HB DISLIKED A MESSAGE

Heather

That whole theory is just asinine.

Regina

Clan Whatshisface believed it was true.

Heather

People in those days also thought 'draining the humors' healed people. Ask me how many times I've done a bloodletting in the ICU?

Zero. Zero is the answer.

1:29pm

Molly

Clan MacGregor of Loch Slochd.

2:12pm

Amelie

You gonna try lunging him today?

Lounging him?

I never know how to spell that.

Molly

If the rain ever stops.

AS LAUGHED AT A MESSAGE

Amelie

So no, you are not.

August 27, 2023

8:34am

Molly

It's a sloppy mess in the round pen. Think he'll
break a leg if I try exercising him today?

Amelie

He's a horse, isn't he?

Heather

Definitely yes. Lol

Regina

Dodger is (mostly) reformed! He'll be
a good boy. I believe in him.

3:42pm

Molly

Guess who is the very bestest horse???

MC FORWARDED A56GH825.JPG

Regina

YAY! *:partyconfetti:*

Molly

The water and mud didn't seem to bother him at all.

Regina

You decide to keep him yet?

Molly

All we did was walk. I'm not deciding anything until
I see if he's walk/trot/canter sound and rideable.

Amelie

She's gonna keep him.

Heather

Yup.

August 29, 2023

8:17pm

Molly

Larry showed up at the house.

Amelie

Did you shut the door in his face??

Regina

I thought you told him to stop harassing you?

Heather

Right @regina !? She said she sent him a cease and desist text. Why is he still bothering her?

9:32pm

Molly

Which vintage goes better with rage? White or red?

Heather

A twelve year pinot noir, for sure.

Amelie

Restraining orders aren't that hard to get...

Regina

You good, Mol?

Molly

I will be. :*wineglass*:

It's five o'clock somewhere, right?

Amelie

It's actually past five here. :*shrug*:

Regina

What did Larry say?

Molly

He wants to get his stuff. One problem, though.
I paid for everything because he couldn't
keep a job for more than two months.

He said he's left a bunch of messages (which I deleted,
but I didn't tell him that) to try to set up a time.

He won't even tell me what 'stuff' he wants.

I told him to leave or I'd call the cops. He drove off, but said he'll be back.

Amelie

Bonfire? We burn 'his stuff'...then there's no reason for him to contact you.

Molly

He wants the dog.

Heather

Nope. That's not happening.

Molly

I told him over my dead body.

Regina

I like Ame's idea about a restraining order. If he didn't pay for that stuff, he has no right to it. No amount of wishful thinking changes that. And if he can't keep a job, he can't pay for the puppy.

Tell him to get a lawyer.

Molly

Over. My. Dead. Body. :wine-glass:

:wine-glass:

:wine-glass:

August 30, 2023

6:44am

Molly

Uggghhhghgjhgjhgjhjhghghjhhjghgjhgjhgh

8:02am

Heather

The wine got her again.

AS LAUGHED AT A MESSAGE

August 31, 2023

11:00am

Regina

Hangovers were so easy when we were young.

HB LIKED A MESSAGE

AS LIKED A MESSAGE

Regina

Let us know if you need more wine, Mol.

Or company.

Air hugs.

September 2, 2023

7:13am

Molly

Gonna try trotting Dodger today.

10:14am

Heather

How'd it go?

Molly

He was perfect. :hearteyes:

Why can't men be this nice?

Heather

A lot of them are. Just not Larry.

Amelie

Stick with horses.

HB LAUGHED AT A MESSAGE

September 3, 2023

8:52am

Molly

Dodger is out of shape, but we did a few circles of canter in each direction. He's weak and unbalanced, but completely sound! And his drain holes are healed up. Time for a saddle?

Amelie

They don't make saddles that big.

Heather

Ame is right. Lol

Regina

Bareback it is! When are you thinking? One of us should be there to hold him while you lean your weight over him.

(Just in case.)

Amelie

I'm free next weekend.

Regina

Same.

Heather

I'm off tomorrow, if you have the holiday free?

Molly

Yes! I have it off! *:horseracing:*

:hearteyes:

Regina

Wait, you're not using that kelpie bridle, right?
The dead lady's note was specific and clear.

'NO'.

Heather

This again?

Regina

Why take a chance? If he really was a kelpie,
wouldn't putting HIS bridle ON HIM be the same
as 'giving it back'? Then he's in control, right??

Heather

Seriously, Reggie? Lol

Amelie

I've got an old bitless bridle. Pretty sure it'll
fit if we punch a new hole in the leather.

RF LOVED A MESSAGE

Molly

Hmmm, yeah, that might work. Maybe we'll
keep the halter over it, in case he can't
figure out the bitless setup.

Amelie

Welp, next weekend it is!

RF LOVED A MESSAGE

HB LIKED A MESSAGE

4:44pm

Molly

Larry sent a text. Said he's coming over
tomorrow and that I'd 'better let him in or
else'. Too bad for him I changed the locks!

I reminded him that he took 'his stuff'
when he left. I made sure of it!

Heather

What time?

Molly

Afternoon sometime. Said it'll probably
be after the rain stops.

Amelie

So...never.

Heather

You want me to be your backup? I have
no problem telling him to GTFO.

(Or having the police on speed dial.)

Molly

Sure, if you want. Maybe he'll listen if someone
else is there. Witnesses and all that.

Or maybe we can just lock up the house
and take the doggo for a hike.

HB LIKED A MESSAGE

Molly

Nvm, can't leave Dodger home alone...
in case Larry does something stupid.

Heather

Stupid?

Molly

He's a loud and proud NRA member.

Heather

I thought you guys kept the guns locked up?

Molly

He took his when I kicked him out.

HB DISLIKED A MESSAGE

7:21pm

Molly

Larry just left another voicemail. Delete.

9:56pm

Molly

And another voicemail. Delete.

Amelie

WTF?

Regina

You need to get a restraining order,
Mol. That's not normal.

HB LIKED A MESSAGE

AS LIKED A MESSAGE

September 4, 2023

3:52am

Molly

Can't sleep so I'm out in the barn. Already raked the
aisle and cleaned Dodger's stall. Tack room, you're next!

4:39am

Molly

Kelpie bridle is so purty now that it's cleaned up!

MC FORWARDED A56GH905.JPG

5:55am

Molly

@everyone, listen to Dodger's little sleepy
snore when I brush his belly.

MC FORWARDED 4-56421354-5621.MP4

:hearteyes:

Dodger is really the sweetest guy. I know I said not to let me foster fail, but I'm starting to think this is his forever home. That *we* are each other's forever home.

RF LIKED A MESSAGE

Regina

Ha! I knew it!

MC LOVED A MESSAGE

6:12am

HB LOVED A MESSAGE

AS LOVED A MESSAGE

Heather

Bad news, Mol. I got called into work.

Molly

Really?

Heather

I told them I could only do a few hours until they found coverage. I should still be there this afternoon. But if 'Two Pistol Larry' shows up before I get there, don't let him in the house.

10:57am

Molly

Rain is slowing down.

Think I'll do some more work with Dodger. I'm just gonna check to see how the kelpie bridle fits. Maybe do some long lining off of it.

Regina

Just wait until next weekend! Ame will bring the bitless, and we'll be there to help.

11:11am

Regina

At least wait until Heather gets there this afternoon, yeah?

Molly

I'm not gonna ride him. Just trying to keep busy.

Regina

You worried about seeing Larry?

Molly

Yeah. The screaming and the threats...
Makes me nervous, you know?

Regina

Air hugs.

Molly

I was just starting to feel better. More like myself.
Now I gotta deal with Larry's BS again.

Regina

Starting to feel like a strong,
independent woman, you mean?

Molly

*horsewoman

RF LIKED A MESSAGE

11:19am

Molly

Larry just called, @heather. Said he'll be here no
later than 12:30. I hate when he says vague crap
like that. For all I know he's right up the street.

Heather

Okay, leaving now. Should get there around the
same time. DON'T LET HIM IN THE HOUSE.

Regina

> My sister is gonna watch my kids. I'm on
> my way over now, too. Grabbing Ame on
> the way. Hope that's okay, Mol!

Amelie

> No way I'm missing the chance to tell Larry off.

11:25am

Molly

> Dodger in his kelpie bridle! Isn't he the handsomest??

MC FORWARDED A56GH911.JPG

11:31am

Regina

> Just picked up Ame. Be there soon.
> No riding alone, okay Mol?

Heather

> Traffic! ETA is 12:45 now.

Regina

> Mol? No riding, right?

12:02pm

Molly

I mean, a hack around the paddocks isn't really riding, right?

RF DISLIKED A MESSAGE

12:09pm

Molly

Okay, but Dodger is such a peach! He doesn't steer well, but he's definitely been ridden before.

Reminds me of a bombproof kids' horse.

Just keeps plodding along, nice and steady.

Amelie

Duh. Draft horses only have one speed.

Molly

He keeps trying to visit the neighbor's cow field.

At least he's not stealing grass every five seconds. lol

Amelie

Reggie is driving, but she says 'A draft horse? How would kids get on him?'

I told her about visiting the cow field. She swore
and said 'The kelpie controls the bridle!'

RF REPLIED TO A MESSAGE "REMINDS ME OF A BOMBPROOF
KIDS' HORSE."

Doesn't steer well. Keeps rolling tank.

*like a tank. Stupid talk to text.

Or like a river?

Amelie

Ha!

AS FORWARDED TINATURNER.GIF

Also, we hit Heather's traffic. ETA is 12:52 now.
Hopefully Larry's stuck on the highway, too.

Heather

Yup, 12:55 on my GPS.

12:14pm

Molly

Damn, the river next door is angry. Totally overflowed
the banks and took out a corner of the neighbor's
fence. My whole back field is under water.

Like, the river is seriously raging. It's up to Dodger's fetlocks! Guess we got more rain than I thought.

@everyone the weather sucks, and Larry sucks, but it's so nice to be back in the saddle again. I really missed this. I should've never given it up.

I won't make that mistake again.

AS LIKED A MESSAGE

Heather

Horse girls til the end, right?

Molly

Horse girls til the end. :smileface:

Regina

Speaking of Larry, I really hope he doesn't beat us there. Text us if he does, Mol.

12:30pm

Regina

Mol?

12:45pm

Amelie

Mol, you good? This traffic is awful. Another storm

came out of nowhere. Like, seriously, NO WHERE.
A flash flood swept a motorcycle off the highway
and into a VERY deep, VERY watery ditch. Did not
end well for the man on the bike. :motorcycle

:sadface:

Regina

Hoping to get to your place by 1:30ish.

Heather

ETA is 1:37.

12:53pm

Regina

Mol?

Heather

Damn! I just heard more thunder! Will it ever end?

Amelie

Molly? You good?

A Unicorn's Horn Is Proof Against Poison

Clare Packard

Clare Packard has a degree in History from the University of Edinburgh and enjoys drawing inspiration from historical settings and cultures for her fantasy worlds. She's currently working as a librarian, but training for a career in museums and archives so that she can look after 'cool old stuff'. She is a fairytale/folklore nerd and very much enjoys telling old stories anew. When not writing, Clare can usually be found attempting craft projects, bopping to medieval pop song covers, and cheerfully bothering her friends about her latest favourite book.

Lorenzo Delgado allowed himself a grim smile of satisfaction. The plan could not have been going any smoother than if it had been ground into a perfectly fine powder by a pestle. He was glad he came. He had debated whether it would be wise to attend the banquet, given he would be guilty of assassinating the most honoured guest before the first course ended. But his client would likely expect a full report of what happened, and besides, Lorenzo had never not been present to watch one of his targets expire.

The poison was to be slipped in the Queen of England's wine by the woman in the royal kitchens he had seduced. Not that it had taken much convincing for either the poisoning or the seduction. Joan Smith was all too willing to help him. He didn't *technically* need to seduce her, but... she was very pretty, not to mention intelligent. He promised to take her home with him to Spain once the plot was complete. She had been surprised by his offer—moved to tears in fact—but had agreed, much to his delight. He hadn't expected to find love while ensuring a death, but he was glad he had.

Say what you will about the English, he thought with a lopsided smile at all the fine ladies gathered around the banqueting table, *You can't deny they have a fine garden of roses, petals just begging to be opened.* The current queen of England had not arrived yet, but he knew from descriptions and his client that she was a beauty. Porcelain skin, flaming red hair, bewitching eyes...

Funny. He swirled the wine in his goblet. *All this trouble and effort to kill a woman I haven't even laid eyes on.* He took a pensive sip, watching as servants delivered plates of food and a large jug of wine to the head table where the queen would be seated.

Lorenzo took note of the young man standing near the queen's seat. He suffered from the usual facial deformities of the youth, red spots all over his nose and cheeks, but in spite of this, he had a proud countenance.

"The queen has her own personal food-taster," Joan had told him, lying on her side, trailing her fingers across his naked torso. Lorenzo believed the most opportune time to discuss work was at night. And in bed, if his co-conspirator was an agreeable woman. Luckily for him, Joan was of the same opinion. "He's barely out of boyhood. He thinks all the other boys working in the palace are mad with envy that he gets to eat and drink from the queen's own plate."

"An honour to eat from the most beautiful queen in all of Christendom's plate, hm?" he asked sarcastically, gently fondling Joan's breasts.

Joan smiled languidly at him. "More like getting to eat nicer fare every day than most people will ever consume in their lifetimes. Well," she moved closer to him, pressing her body against his, "until he eats or drinks something that disagrees with him."

Lorenzo smiled languidly back. "Now tell me... what other precautions have been taken to ensure the queen does not die from poison?"

"Who says there are other precautions?" Joan answered back teasingly.

Lorenzo tsked. "Joan... there *have* to be more precautions than just a young lad to drop conveniently dead before the queen takes a sip."

"A lowly servant girl like me isn't privy to such secrets," Joan replied with a sigh, turning over in bed, presenting him with the curves of her hips and backside. The assassin bit down hard on his lower lip with desire, admiring her figure. "And even if I did, it would take only the most skilled seducer to entice it out of me."

Lorenzo pressed himself hard against her back, so hard she let out a loud gasp that quickly turned into a moan. "Oh, I think I can manage that, my dulce," he whispered in her ear, grabbing her hips tightly.

The other precaution had turned out to be a piece of a unicorn's horn, dipped into the queen's food and wine. Lorenzo wasn't particularly surprised by this—almost every monarch had their own unicorn horn now, even some of the higher nobility. Finding somebody to supply a fake unicorn horn to replace the real one was difficult. There were plenty of peddlers selling "genuine" unicorn horns to gullible fools willing to part with their money for a carved, painted twig. Eventually, he managed to find a peddler who catered to nobility that were a little less gullible than the rest in that they *knew* what a unicorn horn looked like. Joan, after some more "convincing," which involved passionate embraces in a secluded pantry into the early hours of the morning, had taken the false unicorn horn and switched it with the real one. The false unicorn horn had also been doused liberally in poison, so even if the poisoned wine never met the queen's lips, the poison from the horn, when dipped in an unpoisoned cup of wine or plate of food, would still be enough to send the queen to an early grave.

Poison was more difficult to obtain. Lorenzo did not have much experience with poisons. He had experience with death, too much some would argue, but over the years, he prided himself on developing a certain technique when killing. He knew where to stab a man so he would bleed to death within seconds, throw a dagger at just the right angle so it could pierce the heart easily, how to smoothly slice a sharp dagger across a throat so quickly that a victim was dead before they reached the floor. Most important of all, he knew how to dispatch the target quickly without causing them any pain. Respect for the kill, dignity in the death. He shook his head to think of the suffering his earlier victims could have avoided. It was rather like an artist looking back upon his old work and marvelling at how far he had come, wondering how he could ever have been so clumsy.

While he was confident that he was the master assassin of the knife—the quick stab in the dark—when it came to poisons, he was an utter novice. But killing the queen in his preferred method would be utter madness. Even if it was possible to get close enough to the queen to stab her—unlikely given the utter distrust in England towards Spanish, it was surprising he had even managed to get an invitation to the banquet—she was so closely guarded and surrounded by witnesses, it wouldn't be long before his head hit the executioner's block. Although he'd become an artist of death, he had no interest in becoming a piece of art himself.

So he found a place hidden deep in the sprawling back alleys of the great city. The old shopkeeper had chuckled when Lorenzo told him what he was after.

"Poison, hey?" giving Lorenzo a grin full of spittle and yellowed teeth. "Who are you poisoning then, ya foreign cur? The queen?"

"No, my falcon," Lorenzo replied, turning away to nonchalantly examine the dried herbs hanging from the ceiling and to avoid getting a full face of the shopkeeper's stinking breath. "He caught a disease whilst flying through your overly wet country-side and I must put him down. Does it ever *not* rain in this god-forsaken country?"

"A simple sword to the side would work just as well," the shop-keeper told him, ignoring his question. "Or a shot from one of those newfangled guns."

Lorenzo shook his head. "Too messy."

"Fair enough." The shopkeeper shuffled into the back of the con-fined shop.

"I would prefer a poison that would cause the least amount of suffering to the poor beast," Lorenzo called after him. "Quick and painless."

"Ya don't want much, do ya?" the shopkeeper remarked when he came shuffling back. "This should do the trick. It's hemlock. The bigger the dose the bird can swallow, the quicker he'll fall right off his perch!" he cackled. He handed the dusty, chipped glass bottle, which might have once contained wine in some not-so-distant past, over to the assassin. Lorenzo held it in his palm, feeling its weight before pulling out the cork stopper. His nose recoiled —the poison smelt like... well, poison.

"This is enough to kill a flock, not just a single bird," Lorenzo remarked with a disarming laugh. "By God, it's probably enough to finish off me!"

The old shopkeeper answered with another loud cackle. "More than enough, sir! Only a third of the bottle and you'll be as dead as doornail. Better hope an Englishman doesn't get hold of it, eh?"

Lorenzo's mouth curled upwards into a smirk. "Very much so." He held the bottle to the dim candlelight in the room before turning towards the shopkeeper. "I don't wish to insult your professional knowledge, but I would like to test that a third of this bottle really does cause an instant, painless death. Please," he unsheathed his dagger and pointed the tip at the shopkeeper's wrinkled throat in one smooth motion, "open your mouth wide and *do* remember to swallow..."

The shopkeeper turned out to be quite correct; a third of the bottle did cause instant death. The assassin looked down at the sprawled out body of the shopkeeper, paralysed in the throes of death, his mouth wide open. Lorenzo wasn't exactly satisfied with the result — he didn't like the fear in the frozen eyes of the dead man. The shopkeeper hadn't taken very long to die, but it was still enough for him to know death was approaching and fear it.

Lorenzo hoped the Queen of England would be very thirsty that evening and drink her wine down in one gulp. His employer wanted her to suffer, scorned as he was and desperate for revenge, but the assassin he had hired did not. From Lorenzo's experience, you hired an assassin when you *needed* someone dead, because their existence stood in your way — an inconvenience to get rid of and you were willing to pay for their riddance, much as you would pay a ratcatcher to rid your home of a rat infestation. But if you *wanted* someone dead, you did it yourself. You would choose the most painful method you could think of and relish their suffering as they begged you to forgive them for whatever slight it was that caused you to desperately crave their demise.

Lorenzo pocketed the bottle of poison with a frustrated sigh. He normally refused assassinations of this sort. He dealt with the cold but calculated removal of life, with the least amount of pain involved for the victim, employer, and assassin. When emotion was involved, though, things got messy, and he liked to avoid messy. It was rather like, in fact *too much* like, walking in on a couple or family having a heated argument and one of them turning to you, demanding you help them settle it —and by settle it, they meant take their side against the other.

But Lorenzo needed the protection that only his current employer could provide for him. Unless he wanted to end up lying in a forgotten dead heap in a crumbling back alley. Despite his best efforts (well, not exactly his best efforts if he was being entirely honest with himself, but they were efforts nevertheless), he had managed to find himself in a mess. One that only someone with the amount of power his employer wielded would be able to get him out of, for a price. And that price was the death of a queen.

Just then, it was announced loudly that the queen had entered the banqueting hall. The hall was filled with the sound of chairs being scraped back as guests scrambled to their feet to acknowledge the queen's presence. Lorenzo rose with the rest of them, his expression one of genuine respect for and interest to see the woman he was about to kill.

Queen Elizabeth I of England was a fine woman. An ornamental French hood pushed her glossy red hair back from her face, displaying a proud ivory countenance to her guests. Her velvet gown rustled richly in the respectful silence held by the guests as she walked in. Gold and pearls, symbols of wealth and purity, adorned her attire. Her dark eyes shone with amusement and life as she took her seat at the head table, welcoming them all warmly to the feast.

Lorenzo instinctively started comparing the queen's features with Joan's, and found Joan was in all ways the better beauty in his eyes, apart from the eyes. The queen did have the most bewitching eyes, the kind you ached after whenever you weren't getting lost in their depths. She must have inherited those from her mother. Lorenzo sipped his wine thoughtfully. All the accounts of Anne Boleyn were that she was not much of a beauty, not when compared to the Spanish queen, Catherine of Aragorn, first wife of her father. But still she had charmed him, with her eyes and her wit —and according to some sources, witchcraft. That was certainly what the late king Henry VIII had argued when her mother failed to produce a male heir, only the current queen. At the execution, Anne Boleyn was afforded the honour of a quick death, by a skilled French swordsman.

I would have liked to have met that swordsman. It would have been interesting to meet a man who was as skilled in the art of death as I am, Lorenzo thought to himself, eating his food as though he did not have a care in the world, an innocent not responsible for any crime committed or about to be committed. He watched as the queen's cup was filled to the brim with wine that had been laced with poison. The unicorn horn, he was sure, was nearby...

"Ladies and gentlemen," a clear, resonant voice spoke over the clatter of knives and forks. Lorenzo would have mistaken it for a herald if the speaker hadn't been female. All heads turned towards the queen. Respectful silence reigned once more.

"I have been informed by a trustworthy source that my life is in danger tonight," Queen Elizabeth stated as casually as someone would when discussing the recent weather. There was a chorus of gasps, confused mutters, and a titter of nervous laughter that echoed about the hall. And the cool silent beads of sweat that slowly ran down Lorenzo's forehead. His body began to shiver despite the warm heat of the hall.

"This cup," the queen declared solemnly, lifting it high in the air, "has been filled with poisoned wine. So much poison, I am told, that drinking a mere mouthful would cause me to be lying prostrate across this table, dead." She nonchalantly poured the contents of the goblet onto the banqueting table.

Lorenzo could hardly hear the questions being yelled up around him to the queen. It was rendered to a dull buzzing by his panicking brain. The questions "how?!" and "why?!" and most insistently "what do I do?! what do I *do*?!" were whirling around his head with the force of a storm over the channel.

"My unicorn's horn, which I have as a precaution against such attempts upon my life, has been replaced with a fake and tainted with the same poison as the wine," Queen Elizabeth continued, oblivious to all the shouting and the crisis of her would-be assassin. "My guests, know this..." She rose from her chair. The hall went silent again, enthralled by their queen. "...the next time an assassin *dares* to try poisoning me, they will not be as lucky as the one tonight has been and never set foot in my palaces, let alone spoil my food. But even if they should turn out to be that persistent, they will still not succeed. For your queen has for her protection a creature as pure of heart and spirit as herself."

The queen waved her hand regally to the guards manning the entrance doors. The doors were swung open. All the guests leaned forward like the audience at a play, hanging on the edge of their seats, knowing a climax is coming, but not sure what to expect.

Lorenzo's heart threw itself into his mouth. He gripped the sides of his chair, nails digging into the arms. The small part of his mind that was still thinking rationally was informing him that what was entering the hall couldn't possibly be real. But it was very hard to deny all his other senses telling him it was.

It was a unicorn.

The unicorn slowly trotted into the hall, each clip-clop of its golden hooves echoing off the walls. Its coat was as white and clean as freshly fallen snow, its mane and tail sparkling as though its hair had been made of polished crystals. A horn, swirled upwards into a sharp point, gleamed pearlescent in the candle-light. Many guests lowered their heads in awe as the unicorn passed by them. Even Lorenzo forgot his fear for a moment, his heart swelling with a joy he did not properly understand as he watched the magnificent creature.

The unicorn stopped in the middle space between the tables, right in front of where Lorenzo was sitting. Slowly, it bent down on one front foreleg, kneeling. The unicorn lowered its head respectfully towards the queen, its horn tapped against the stone paving with a gentle ringing sound.

Queen Elizabeth inclined her head respectfully back to the unicorn. "Noble creature, synonymous with the virtues of grace and purity this queen herself embodies, you are welcome to court. Arise." The unicorn did so. It stood to attention, like one of the queen's guards awaiting an order, which it was soon given. "Could you please reveal the identity of my would-be killer?"

Lorenzo's heart clenched as the unicorn turned its head towards him. The unicorn flicked its ears indifferently as it pointed its horn like a sword at the assassin drenched in an anxious sweat. A cry went up across the tables, men reaching for their weapons, while the women screamed or grabbed the cutlery aggressively.

Lorenzo moved instinctively, adrenaline urging him to do something to save his worthless hide. His chair clattered to the ground as he pushed it away, running past all the guests who were a lot slower than him. He took out his dagger and quickly stabbed the servants trying to block his exit out of the open door. The banqueting hall was miles away from any entrance into the palace, only accessible through a maze of convoluted corridors full of servants and guards. There was, however, a great number of windows...

Well, Lorenzo thought to himself as he heard the clamour of footsteps and furious shouts behind him, *I've never jumped out of a window before. Might be fun.*

He had just managed to pry a window open with his dagger when he registered a presence behind him. It wasn't a menacing or threatening presence, but he felt the weight of its power on his back. And its judgement. He turned.

The unicorn was gazing at him with an enigmatic expression. Lorenzo stood there, frozen in place. The creature was even more majestic up close. *So beautiful,* Lorenzo thought with breathless wonder, like a man seeing stars for the first time. *This must be what meeting an angel feels like.*

Cold air hit his back, waking him from his reverie. *Escape, you fool, don't gawk at the unicorn like it's a pretty girl!* He opened the window as wide as it could go and prepared himself to hit the ground hard below...

Except he never even made it out of the window because just then pain exploded in his back, causing him to fall back from the window onto the corridor floor with a cry. *That was not a very professional thrust,* Lorenzo thought irritably as he clutched his side, watching the blurred figures of guests with their swords drawn coming down the corridor towards him. *This pain is quite unnecessary. Easily avoidable if you know what you're doing.*

Lorenzo glanced upwards. The unicorn's horn, once pearly white, now had a glistening ruby sheen to it. *Oh well.* Unconsciousness was closing in fast, and the world was growing further and further away from him. *I can chalk it up to inexperience. Unicorns are probably not used to killing.*

***

Lorenzo woke up, very confused, in a very comfortable bed, in what was very much *not* a barren prison cell. It looked very similar to the guest chamber he'd been staying in in the city, with its neat but sparse decor. He touched his hand to where he'd been stabbed by the unicorn's horn. A bandage was neatly wrapped around his wound.

He groggily lifted himself up from the bed, wincing at the waves of pain that crashed down across his muscles as he did so. *Shouldn't I be? I'm not complaining, but... shouldn't I be dead? Isn't that how assassins who are discovered are normally treated? Is it some weird English custom that requires them to heal a criminal before they execute them?*

The door to his room banged open. A small child, a girl of around six or seven, came barging in.

"Hello!" the girl shouted up at him. "Mama said I could bring you downstairs if you were awake. *Are* you awake?"

Well, I am now. Lorenzo's sore head pounded with the girl's loud voice throbbing through his ears. "Yes, young lady, I am."

"Good!" The girl grabbed him by the hand and dragged him from the room, leading him God-knows-where. Just as Lorenzo suspected, it was a townhouse somewhere in the metropolis. They passed several servants, but none of them paid him any heed.

"My name is Anne. What's your name?" The girl reminded him vividly of an enthusiastic puppy that had been taken out on their first walk, yipping at everything and everyone.

"Lorenzo."

"Lor-en-zo." The little girl sounded out his name thoughtfully. "Lor-en-zo. You have a very pretty name, Lor-en-zo. I wish my name was as pretty as yours."

"Anne is a very pretty name," Lorenzo responded. "It means 'grace,' having beauty and charm without effort. And you are very beautiful and charming."

Anne giggled loudly, causing the assassin to smile. Lorenzo wondered when the last time he had heard such a pleasant, innocent sound before.

The girl stopped outside a door and knocked hard with her small fist. "Mother! I have brought the man to see you!"

"Bring him in, dearest," Came a voice behind the door, a voice Lorenzo recognised.

He stared in disbelief as he opened the door and found a woman sitting at a small writing desk. A fine lady with a velvet yellow dress fit for the queen he tried to kill. A golden belt with rubies embedded along the chain was the only accessory the lady wore. Her hair was swept back, pinned up high into a bun. From her appearance it was clear she was a person of some circumstance. Just like when she had been wearing a simple linen dress and a shawl, he had thought her to be a person of little circumstance.

But in both cases, Lorenzo thought, as the lady turned around in her chair and met his eyes, *I have thought her to be one of the most beautiful ladies that I've ever seen.*

"Thank you, Anne," the woman Lorenzo knew as Joan Smith said to her daughter. "Now run along to your tutor. You're late for your Latin lessons. And I have business to discuss with Mister Lorenzo Delgado here."

"Yes, mother." Anne asked, kissing her on the cheek, "Is Lor-en-zo going to be staying with us long? I like him."

"I like him too. But the decision to stay will be entirely up to him. Now go." The little girl hurried out of the room, giving Lorenzo a quick hug before she left.

"Your daughter is learning Latin?" Lorenzo asked curiously as the door closed behind him.

"She is. It forms a root to most of our language and those of our neighbours," Joan responded, quickly finishing what she was writing before they came in. "Anne has quite a talent for languages and I want to encourage that."

"Very wise."

Feeling both awkward and strangely calm, Lorenzo sat down on an empty chair near the desk. The window was open, and the scent of flowers and herbs wafted in amongst the usual smells of the city. The townhouse clearly backed onto a well-tended garden.

"So," he asked, while she scratched her quill against the parchment, "is your name Joan Smith?"

"No." She finished what she was writing and turned to smile at him. "It is Joanne Mildmay."

"Joanne," he repeated. "Close, but not too close."

"I like to make it easier for myself to remember," Joanne responded with a shrug of her shoulders. "I take it you've realised what's happened."

Lorenzo nodded. "I recognise I have been tricked by a very skilled professional in my own field. An equal, if not superior." He bowed towards her. "How did you come into the Queen's service?"

"I was once one of the queen's servants—well, I still am a servant of the queen in my current work—and I found that as both a servant and a woman, I could see and hear things to her advantage. She asked her spymaster, Francis Walsingham, to recruit me into his service. He was reluctant at first. There are already several servants in the spymaster's employ, but he agreed once he discovered I had a proficiency for gardening, specifically in the tending and extraction of poisonous plants." She smirked. "And for sneaking them into the foods and drinks of victims undetected."

"The King of Spain should have hired you, then," Lorenzo commented. "My assassination skills lie chiefly in the blade, not the cup, but he hired me anyway."

Joanne's eyes narrowed. "Why did King Phillip insist upon poisoning?"

"He wanted the queen to suffer before she died—because of how she slighted his advances—and thought poison would help achieve that more than a blade would. I believe in clean death, painless and quick. And it did not see what the queen had done to warrant such a painful death."

"Which is why you decided on hemlock, and in such a large

quantity." Lorenzo nodded. "But why did you agree to the assassination if you're not confident with poisons?"

Lorenzo sighed. "At the time, I was in a position that made it impossible for me to refuse the king's request."

"Ah, a man with a vice." Joanne propped up her elbow upon the desk. "Well, what was it?"

"Guess."

"Gambling. Too much time at the card tables."

"No."

"Family troubles. You needed the money to pay off some debt."

"The only trouble I have with family is that I haven't got any."

"Oh, that is sad. Hm. You killed the wrong person! An assassination gone wrong!"

"Wrong again. Really, my dulce, I thought you would be better at guessing than this," Lorenzo responded, watching with some amusement at Joanna's exasperated facial expression.

"The English will surrender to the Spanish, just this once. Tell me, please."

Lorenzo awkwardly fiddled with his bandage, not meeting her eyes. "I slept with the wrong woman," he confessed. "My one true vice, making love to beautiful women I shouldn't."

"Oh, I don't know," Joanne remarked softly. There was an undercurrent of bittersweetness in her tone that made Lorenzo glance upwards. "Perhaps it's a case of circumstances, being there at the wrong time..."

"Her husband certainly was."

Joanne laughed. "Ah, husbands. They can be a pain for a woman to manage, in my experience. Anne's father was a suspected traitor to the queen, but none of the other spies could find any hard evidence of it, namely because his properties were very well-guarded. The spymaster set me up as a lady with a false background and instructed me to seduce him, to earn the traitor's trust. The queen said that if I could find the evidence, I could keep his money, his properties, his title..." She gestured around to the walls of the townhouse and expensive furnishings. "*Everything*, as a reward for my service. Not a bad bargain for a girl who came from the streets." Her face fell pensive.

"But it was too high a price?" Lorenzo guessed cautiously.

Joanne sighed. She pulled out the hair pins, freeing her shiny, chestnut hair from her bun, letting it fall across her shoulders. She looked more like the carefree, feisty servant girl Lorenzo had fallen for. He noticed for the first time how the dress, despite its fine quality, sat ill upon her shoulders.

"I gained my daughter, Anne. She is worth more than all my late husband's properties and wealth put together. *She* made everything I did worth it." Joanne's hands were shaking. Lorenzo reached out and took them in his instinctively. "I wooed him, I married him, I managed his household, I appealed to his ego, I agreed to everything he said in public or private, I was cloistered alone inside one house to the next for months on end like a nun, I spent time in his bed... It took two years and the birth of a child before he decided to trust me, and the evidence I was after dropped into my lap. I poisoned him the week after Anne was born, and I was out of confinement. I didn't want to waste any more years of my life as his wife, his prisoner. And I didn't want my daughter to join me in my living hell. The reward I received could never compensate what I endured."

Lorenzo kissed her forehead. "You have suffered so much, my *dulce*. I would have relieved you of it sooner if I had known."

"Ah, but then I would not have found the evidence that gave me this position." She smiled up at him. "And I would not be a spy and we would not have met."

"Hm. True," Lorenzo admitted. "Which reminds me I must ask, what is to become of me? Am I to be executed? Imprisoned?"

"Ah, well, that depends on you." Joanne picked up the piece of paper from her desk and handed it over to him. She got up from her seat and made herself comfortable on Lorenzo's lap. "What do you think?"

"Let me finish reading first," Lorenzo hushed her. It was an interesting document to be sure, but it was hard to focus on when Joanne was nestling herself against his chest and brushing her lips against his neck.

"Pass me the quill," he said when he had finished reading the letter.

Joanne raised her eyebrows. "Just like that?" She got up and fetched him a quill. "You do know you'll never be able to return to Spain again, don't you?"

Lorenzo shrugged. "Given I'll be killed the moment I step off the ship, it's not a great loss. Besides, I have no family to tie me there. And I do need protection." He signed off on the contract. "And besides," he added, pulling Joanne back onto his lap. "I think I'd rather enjoy working with you. My dulce poisoner."

"My perfect swordsman." Joanne gave him a kiss. "The queen

was quite impressed, you know. She was sad about the death of her servants, of course, but she was unable to deny the skill with which they had been dispatched. It was easy to convince her to offer you the position of personal assassin." She stopped, drawing back from him in a serious tone. "And I wanted you. Initially I thought you were just using me to gain access to the queen, but when you made me that offer to come with you, I... I felt wanted. I felt loved. I hadn't felt something so pure, so beautiful for a very long time." She brushed his hair out of his face. "And I've always wanted someone who can understand the work I do."

"So have I," Lorenzo answered, holding her close to him. "I would be happy to make you feel wanted and loved your whole life," he expressed sincerely.

Joanne let out a giggle, blushing. "Did you say that beautiful women are your vice, or that *you* are the vice of beautiful women?"

Lorenzo did not get the chance to reply because just then there was a loud, urgent knocking on the door. Lorenzo and Joanne barely had enough time to pull apart and compose themselves before Anne came bursting into the room.

"Mama, mama! Is it true?!"

"Is what true, my darling?"

"That there was a unicorn at the queen's banquet last night! Tutor told me that it saved the queen's life!" The little girl was practically vibrating with excitement. "Is it true? Was the unicorn real? Tutor said he wasn't sure and to ask you."

"Why not ask Lorenzo? He was there, after all," her mother responded, turning towards him.

Lorenzo had quite forgotten about the unicorn. It had certainly *seemed* real. He placed a hand over the spot where the horn had penetrated his flesh. And felt real.

"It looked like a unicorn," he eventually told Anne. "It was the most beautiful creature I had ever beheld. Save for your mother, of course." The last comment caused Joanne to laugh and Anne to giggle. He picked the little girl up and sat her on his lap, embracing her. He then turned towards Joanne. "But as to whether it was real, I don't know. But I think your mother might."

"Was it real, Mother?" Anne asked again eagerly, looking at her mother with wide eyes. Lorenzo also raised an eyebrow at Joanne, for he too was curious to know the answer.

"I think it might have been real," Joanne answered with an enigmatic smile. "It was certainly quite magical the way it knew who the person trying to kill the queen was. A unicorn only helps those who are pure of heart, like the queen."

Regardless of whether the unicorn was real, the message sent to the kingdom and the rest of Christendom was clear: The Queen of England was pure of heart, a virgin, virtuous, and would not be easily defeated. The unicorn's presence last night was a symbol, and a powerful one at that.

"And the queen is very fond of horses," Anne interjected. "You told me so."

"Indeed she is," Joanne said. "She is very fond of riding; it is not considered a very ladylike pursuit, but the queen is not most ladies."

"I would like to learn to ride," Anne said enthusiastically.

"I can teach you how to ride," Lorenzo offered, watching as the girl's face lit up with delight.

"On a unicorn?!"

"I was thinking more along the lines of a horse. Unicorns can be hard to come by and their horns can be sharp. You have to be careful not to get impaled." He grimaced as Anne accidentally touched his wound. Joanne saw his pain and beckoned Anne onto her own lap.

"I don't suppose when you're not teaching my daughter how to ride, you can teach me how to wield a sword? And a dagger?" Joanne asked, with a gleam in her eyes. "I've always wanted to learn how to do that."

"Only if you share your... gardening expertise in return," Lorenzo responded.

"And I can teach you both Latin and *everything* I know about unicorns!" Anne exclaimed gleefully.

"Well," Lorenzo said, ruffling Anne's hair and sharing a secret smile with Joanne over the top of the little girl's head, "I would certainly like to learn more about unicorns."

High To Kolob On A Cosmic Clydesdale

Katrina Carruth

Katrina Carruth is a chaotic neutral writer, wife, and mother. She is obsessed with writing, cooking, horror, D&D, reading, coffee, rum, Nancy Drew games, tarot, and her delightfully weird family.

When I went to Sadie Chip's stupid new moon crystal party and hesitantly told the universe that I was "ready to witness its power," I didn't think a Clydesdale would show up in my living room at 3AM. At least, I think it was a Clydesdale. It was friggin' huge so, whatever.

I don't know how it got into my house as no windows were broken and no doors had been busted down. But, at such an ungodly hour, I was more concerned with how to get it out. I don't like horses, never been on one, and all I know is that they kick when they're scared. It didn't seem like it would scare easily as it appeared to be uninterested in budging. I don't blame it. I just had the carpets redone. They're nice and plush, but not intended for horses. I tried explaining this to the horse, but it made some snuffing noise that either meant it didn't understand me or didn't care. What I wanted it to say was, "Oh, so sorry about the carpet, let me be out of your hair straight away. Whinny whinny, snuff snuff, whinny." Or something like that as I wasn't really sure what response to expect from a horse.

So, I exited through the front and ran around my unit to the sliding glass doors off the patio hoping the horse would gallop its massive ego right out. But by the time I got them open, the horse was gone. Not even a smudge of stenchy stool left behind.

I thought I'd gone a bit crazy or dreamed it, and I'll admit I had a tad more wine with dinner than usual, but I know what I fucking saw. One does not simply wake up to a Clydesdale in their living room, start talking to it, and go back to bed having imagined the whole thing.

Well, maybe they do, but I don't because, get this: it came back. I opted not to tell anyone about the first time it happened because I didn't need anyone asking when I was going to find a therapist in this new town or if I'm getting settled okay or express some concern about how I've yet to make any real friends or open up about my family and why I moved in the first place or point out that I rarely leave my house to go somewhere besides work or the grocery store (Which was unfair considering I've gotten takeout, not delivery, like thrice since moving here).

But when it showed up the second time, I *lost* it. I'd unintentionally fallen asleep on the couch and woke to a deep, guttural neigh right above my head.

I sat up, cussed it out while searching for my cell phone as it kept neighing like I should know how to interpret it. I tried calling Sadie since she's the woo woo one who got me into this mess but, surprise surprise, the bitch didn't answer. Probably sleeping soundly or busy riding her own manifested horse. I yelled at it and jokingly said if it didn't leave, I'd call IKEA to come pick it up and, holy fuck, it's like it knew about the meatballs. Its eyes got all wide, body completely stiff like it was threatening me.

Obviously, I was scared shitless. There wasn't anywhere else for it to go as the living room's vaulted ceilings provided the only space it wouldn't have to duck or crawl. *Can horses crawl?* So, I slipped off the back of the couch and scurried to the safety of the lower ceilings. The horse thing didn't budge, just stared at me like some cowardly creep. Lucky for me, I'm used to dodging cowardly creeps. So, I snuck off to bed.

It was gone when I woke up.

Before I'd even clocked in at work, I charged to Sadie's desk.

"How do I get the horse out of my house?" I demanded.

"I'm sorry? The what?" she asked, blinking stupidly as she took a gulp of her usual protein shake.

"The horse. The one I manifested—"

"Why did you try to manifest a horse? You live in a condo..."

"—it's been showing up in my living room for the past two nights, right at 3AM—"

"Ooooh, the witching hour!" She wiped her lips.

"—and you need to tell me how to, I dunno, un...manifest...something. Or something." I scowled. Heat rose all the way up into my ears every second that dimwitted smile stayed plastered to her face. "Why are you smiling?" My tone radiated above the cubicles.

"Oh." Her features snapped to a stiff, slightly confused expression. "Sorry. A horse? Aren't you a bit old to be asking the universe for a pony?"

"What? I didn't ask it for a horse. I said I was ready to witness its power since, I dunno, everyone at the party seemed to think it was pretty capable."

"Well, it is." She leaned in, eyes widening, nodding aggressively like confirming a long-suspected secret. "Where's the crystal I gave you?"

The crystal? Was she fucking serious? "I...I...it's..."

She let out a disappointed sigh that sounded uncomfortably like my mother's. "You threw it away, didn't you?"

I forgot about the crystal. "Look, Sadie..."

She threw her hands in the air and swiveled in her chair for an extra dose of disappointed flair. "If you didn't want to come to that party and take it seriously you should have stayed home."

I hadn't expected her to make this so difficult. "I didn't know what a new moon party even was!" A few squeaks from various office chairs alerted me to keep my voice down, so I dropped to a harsh whisper. "Don't pretend you didn't invite me out of pity anyway."

Sadie did not get the talk softer memo. "Well, I wouldn't have had to if you'd try getting to know your coworkers instead of sulking around all day. I was just trying to help you since you've made it crystal clear you're all alone but won't tell anyone why."

I couldn't believe what I was hearing. First of all, my life is none of her business. And second: I just need to get this fucking thing out of my house, and instead she's scolding me about my attitude?!

She exhaled, closed her eyes, annoyingly focused on her breaths as I processed just how late I now was for work. "Can you retrieve the crystal?" she asked, changing the subject.

"Why do I need to retrieve the crys—"

"Becaussssse," she hissed, clearly agitated. At least she was acting like she believed me. "If you did it right, put all your energy into that precious, *expensive*, citrine...God, I don't even want to know what kind of energy you'd be attracting after doing a new moon ritual and then throwing that shit right in the trash. That's a whole other level of..." She waved her hands, jerking them in every direction as if her point was somewhere off in the distance. "...just...just..." Sadie pinched her fingers together, likely imagining me getting crushed between them. "Can you get the crystal back?"

I bit my lip. "No."

She stared, unblinking, unamused. "Well, if you can't get the crystal back because you felt the need to *really* get rid of it, your only other option is to try and ride it."

I nearly choked on my spit. "What?"

She leaned back in her chair and crossed her arms condescendingly across her chest. "Get on the horse. See what happens."

I could not believe what I was hearing. "Let me get this straight..."

She perked up, placed her hands on her thighs—trapped in tight, chaotically patterned, pyramid scheme leggings—like she was about to give a toddler her full attention.

I groaned. "My options are either to rush to the dumps and find some tiny, apparently very expensive, crystal that I supposedly poured my energy into..." She nodded; lips pursed. "Or you want me to be ready at 3AM and figure out how to get on some horse that magically appears in my living room?"

She leaned in again, this time lowering her voice. She beckoned me to strain my back and join her. "You asked the universe to show you its power, right?"

I grudgingly nodded.

"Well, it apparently wants to show you, despite how shitty you were to it." She looked me up and down like the snooty shop-keeper in Pretty Woman. "So, get on and go for a ride. See where it takes you."

Desperate to get out of there, I rushed a halfhearted thank you to Sadie and heard a peppy "Giddy up" as I walked away feeling like the least insane participant of that conversation.

That night, I took a bath, put on my flannel pajamas and boots—well, Uggs. They're comfortable!—and settled into the couch with a jacket tied around my waist, just in case. I considered throwing all my belongings into my backpack for the "just in case" anxiety of this plan, but the thought of throwing my whole life into a single bag yet again was a little "too soon." The point of getting this condo—and the less than savory way I opted to find the cash—was so I didn't have to do that anymore. And now there's a horse threatening to yank me from all my hard work. If I asked the universe to show me its power and it decided to show me how easily it can snip my dreams from my grasp, then the universe and all its precious crystals can go straight to hell.

Like clockwork, the 3AM neigh woke me from my sleep.

Not wanting to give it any immediate satisfaction, I decided not to move much at first. I leaned back to get a good look at the thing. I hated to admit it was pretty stunning, and thankfully showed up odorless.

I guess it wasn't entirely impossible for the horse to be a hal-lucination. So, I took a deep breath, reached out my hand, and pressed a finger gently to the base of its neck.

I gasped at the unexpected sensation. Sure, horses have hair, and I can see it plain as day. But it didn't feel like hair. Not in the way I'd expect from livestock, anyway. It felt more like tiny little worms writhing back and forth so slowly I could barely make out their movement, like plunging my finger into a sleeping pile of maggots.

The texture made absolutely no sense, but horses aren't supposed to just appear in one's house with no sign of entry either, so I wasn't sure what to make of it. Especially once I realized I couldn't pull my finger away. It'd become attached somehow, slowly sucking the rest of me toward it. My whole hand planted against its neck against my will as the tiny whatever-the-hell hair strands pulled my body up off the couch, taking my arm across its neck as the rest of me slithered up its back via the force of some fleshy, unsavory magnetic pull.

I wanted to puke.

My body, compressed against the entire back and neck of the horse, was eventually made half free as my torso and head released from its clutches, allowing me to breathe and sit upright without the feeling of squishy strands against my lips.

*Get on the horse...*of course Sadie would tell me to do something so stupid. If what's already happened is any indication of what's to come, I'm dreading it.

With a sharp kick and a harsh, guttural neigh, a thundering crack echoed through my condo, shattering the walls and sending my few but precious belongings flying into the ether appearing around us.

A single, sparkling road sign appeared as if quickly assembled by falling stars, proudly displaying a single destination: Kolob.

"Fuck," I shouted. "This is a dream, this is a dream, none of this is real..."

The horse bound past the sign at an alarming speed, my hair billowing in messy waves behind me as if desperate to abandon ship. I tried to wriggle myself free, to kick my legs away from the thing. What's that stupid saying? Shoot for the moon or some shit and if you fail you'll land among the stars? Landing among the stars and dying alone in an oblivion of nothingness still felt eons better than making it to our destination. If this was really happening and God was waiting for me, I guess I was technically ready for our meeting. I'd rehearsed it a million times, though I never assumed I'd actually get the chance to spit my wrath in his face. Being that I'd decided I didn't believe in the guy and all...

Asked the universe to see its power and God shows up. What a mess.

The horse galloped through a shimmering archway, up crystalline steps, and abruptly stopped once inside an over-the-top throne room looking place. I was suddenly thankful to be glued to the thing as I would have been thrown off by its sudden ceasing of movement. Though, my neck will never recover from the whiplash.

"Greetings," a man said from a wildly unnecessary desk elevated by twirling clouds. The horse's hairs—if we're calling them that—released me before I knew what was happening, sending me sliding straight to the floor in a clumsy thump. Not my finest moment. And, not that I was hoping to give God my best, but getting myself off the floor with throbbing knees and a mess of confusion in my brain proved to be more frustrating than how I'd always hoped to confront him. "How art thou, my child?" His eyes sparkled with a kindness I hadn't expected.

"Uh...um..." I stammered and shot my fingers into my temples, hoping that a violent flogging would wake me from this terribly realistic dream.

The guy that was apparently God cleared his throat and leaned forward. "I said, how art thou—"

"I heard you," I shouted. "I mean, what the hell—"

"Language!" he boomed.

"—kind of dream is this? Ugh, am I dead?" I groaned, panicking slightly that the last thing I managed to do before dying was go to a new moon crystal party. "I thought people only saw you when they died. So..." I lost track of my thoughts as others gathered around, some I recognized from tattered photos hung in my childhood church. Others from pictures scattered in genealogy books my parents insisted I memorize and idolize. I pinched my skin as hard as I could, allowing the pain to increase until my eyes watered, bringing me to the unfortunate conclusion that I was not dreaming. My words caught in my throat as if afraid to come all the way up. "If I'm not here for some bull"—*Cough*—"bullshit judgment day..." Outraged gasps filled the space. "I'd like to wake up or go home or whatever."

The kindness in his eyes faded to something flat and lifeless, revealing himself as the vacant creature I'd always imagined him to be. Dismissing my outrage (typical), he said, "Did you or did you not attend a blasphemous ritual of occult tomfoolery?"

I couldn't help but laugh, and made a mental note to tell Sadie what God called her party. "Um yup. Sure did." Disgusted grumbles erupted from the audience. "I mean, look at me." I backed up and tugged on my flannel pajamas. "A shining example of occult tomfoolery."

The crowd stiffened their postures as if trapped in some weird group self-flagellation to keep from expressing anything other than disdain for my behavior.

"Dost thou find this funny?" God demanded, standing up from his chair and towering over his already ginormous desk.

I took another step back, taking in the breadth of space he insisted on occupying as he made this massive room suddenly feel much smaller than it was. What a prick. I cleared my throat to keep it from cracking. "I do," I said, keeping my face as straight as possible. "You can probably stop with the whole 'thou' business as nobody really talks like that anymore—"

"I shall speak as I please!" he boomed again. He seemed to really enjoy booming his voice. All these years alive and he acted like a child.

"Ok, well, same..." I offered my signature whoops-a-daisy-you-tried-to-keep-me-brainwashed-but-turns-out-I'm-just-a-regular-millennial shrug. "And..." I opted to fill the silence and thwart his attempt to make me uncomfortable. "While we're on the subject of speaking, I'd like to say that I really, really want to go home now."

"And willst thou change thy ways?" he cocked his head.

"Um, what ways?" I asked. "You mean my occult tomfoolery?"

He rolled his eyes. "Yes. Among other things."

Oh, god. Here we go. "What other things?" I was either going to really regret or be thoroughly entertained by his answer.

His disappointed sigh shook the entire room, so powerful I wouldn't doubt it could be felt on earth, while he whipped out a tattered looking scroll. Apparently, whoever kept track of my plethora of sins regularly has to update it. "In no particular order," his voice rumbled. "Cursing, unfaithfulness, improvidence, hatred of god..." He paused and looked up as I chuckled and didn't continue until I ceased my disrespect. "Lack of natural affection, lustfulness, infidelity—"

"Ok," I shouted and held up my hand. "Hold on. I hardly consider texting a crush while technically having an online girlfriend when I was *thirteen* 'infidelity.' I mean, come on, I haven't had a real relationship in my whole life—"

His volume drowned my own. "—indiscretion, backbiting, whispering, lack of truth, quarrelsomeness, unthankfulness, inhospitality, deceitfulness..." It started to feel like those commercials listing the harmful side effects of some intense prescription drug. "...irreverence, arrogance, pride, profanity—"

"How is that different from cursing?"

"—slander—"

"Wha? Who? Or Whom? Whomst did I slander?"

"—covenant breaking, filthiness, impurity, slothfulness, idolatry—"

"I hardly consider one new moon ritual to fall into idolatry—"

"—blasphemy, denial of god, Jesus Christ, and the Holy Ghost—"

"Wait, is Jesus here?!"

"—Sabbath breaking, envy, jealousy, malice, vengefulness, spite, evil speaking, disobedience to parents—"

I rolled my eyes. I mean, he's not wrong, but he's got to really be stretching the things I've done in my life to make them count for all this shit. I haven't even been away from home long enough to have gone real hard on any of these...except for the disobedience to parents but let's be real here, they were really stepping on the free will god supposedly handed out to everyone...

"—anger, hate, heresy, abomination, insatiable appetite—"

"Well, yeah, the food was super boring growing up. Pretty sure it was you who said, 'man cannot live on bread alone' am I right?"

"That's not what that meant, Child," he hissed and carried on with his sin reading as though it were the most exciting thing on his agenda. "Masturbation—"

Ah! He's getting to the good stuff.

"—petting, fornication, homosexuality, premarital sex, and theft." He glared at me over the scroll. I wasn't sure what I was supposed to do now. Bow? Beg? "How do you wish to repent?"

I choked back a laugh. "Wait, what? Repent? There's not going to be any sort of discussion about some of these pretty outlandish accusations?"

"So, you deny such charges?"

"Deny? No. But—"

"How do you wish to repent?"

Fury rose from my fluttering stomach, into my chest, and rested on my cheeks. I could sense an all too familiar sensation of shame. Of wanting to beg for forgiveness and pretend I didn't have wants and needs of my own; wants and needs that I'd been taught to believe made me a bad person rather than a gloriously nuanced human being. I spent too many years feeling like this. Feeling like I should contort every aspect of my being into an impossible shape to please people who were not capable of it either.

"I'm afraid your soul is on the line, Child. Repenting now and fully committing to rejoining that which you know to be true..." He paused and spread his arms out as if holding up the entire kingdom of heaven for me to see. As if I'd somehow missed it on the way in. "...For the rest of your time on earth is the only way to ensure your salvation."

Wrath whirled like a rabid bat in my chest. "I'm not worried about my salvation," I said through gritted teeth.

Gasps whooshed from the stands. "I beg your pardon?" he asked.

"I said I'm not concerned about my salvation," I shouted, making sure to channel the enthusiasm my bishop had when showing us the piece of gum meant to represent us pure, perfect little girls. I remember the way he chomped and spit as he spewed his lies, the smile on his face as he pulled it from his lips and asked if any of us wanted it. We all grimaced and shrunk back in our chairs, committing to ourselves and our most precious god in that moment to never become a chewed-up piece of gum that nobody would want.

But I'm not a hacked up, slobbery piece of gum, and nobody should ever be made to feel like one.

Well, except the asshole trying to get me to feel some sort of way about my salvation—that I'm assuming includes landing my ass back here in this inhospitable arena. I'd be more than happy to chew him up and stick him someplace where everyone can just forget he exists.

"Fine," he said, crunching the scroll in his fist. Just then, a movement in the crowd caught my eye. A singular figure shuffling in her seat, unable to keep herself from nervously fidgeting to the front of the mob. Oh my god... "Mom?" I shouted, pointing directly at her.

"I'd like a word alone with my daughter," she said, lips quivering.

"You mean my daughter?" God did his little boom boom boom with his voice again.

"Oh, right, yes of course," she whimpered, her frail figure trembling. "Might I have a word alone with her?"

He *hmphed* but seemed annoyed enough with me to allow her request as he snapped his fingers, clearing the room of everyone except my mother and me.

We shouted at the same time, "What the heck is going on?"

"You tell me!" I demanded. "Are you dead?"

Her eyes darted away from mine, lips softening and still trembling. "Yes."

I'd rather have someone punch me in the gut. I know I chose to leave. Chose to take her savings hidden around the house with the justification that she'd never have the guts to use it anyways. But a whole community of people keeping my own mother's death from me was still a lot. Too much.

I didn't know what to say. I should apologize for taking the money and leaving without a word. But she would have tried to stop me, and it probably would have worked. There's no way I could have held those empty cans of cash while looking her in the eye to say goodbye. But I was never going to live a life of my choosing by staying. Was never going to break away from incessant indoctrination about how I, as a woman, was destined to forever serve and satiate those who would do their damnedest to keep me small and obedient.

"Why'd he send a horse?" I asked, not really sure what else to say that wouldn't circle back to me being forced to apologize.

She blinked for several seconds as if attempting to process the last question she expected me to ask. "Well, I told him to send one."

"Why?"

"You always wanted a horse. When you were younger, I mean. I thought for sure you'd get right on it. Didn't think it'd take you so long. I guess I must have been wrong." Her voice trailed off as she eyed her shoes.

My heart sunk to the depths of my gut. "Mom?" I said, pulling her attention back up to me. Time to be honest, I guess. "I never liked horses. I just wanted one because I always imagined myself riding one away from that...cult."

She winced. She always did whenever someone insinuated her controlled, curated life was anything other than a brilliant star that would save her soul. For the first time ever, I felt I could really see her as someone other than my mother. A woman desperate for a sense of belonging, with no tools to understand her unhappiness came from the fear she had in her own curiosity. Someone who chose to believe that happiness awaited her in the afterlife as hell proved to be the definition of her mortal existence.

"Will you repent? So you can be with us?" She held out her hand and I backed away. Tears welled in her eyes. "You can't be with us forever unless you choose us."

I closed my eyes and fought back my own tears. I've fought these tears my whole life. The ones that offered my mother and this entire charade sympathy. "I don't want this."

Her face changed, morphed from devastation straight to dismay. Her nostrils flared as she said, "We'll just find another way to bring you back."

I took another step away from her. "And I'll find another way to leave."

She held her hand back out, forcefully this time, as she'd done so many times when she grabbed it rather than giving me the choice of taking it. I cleared my throat. "You could bring me back a thousand times, and I will say no every single time."

"But you know the truth now—"

"No. This is yours. It's not mine. I don't know what I believe. But it sure as shit isn't this." I hated that it sounded insane, even to me, to deny something while being confronted with it. But I'd always wanted to believe there was more than what I'd been taught, and I refused to let this moment convince me there wasn't something better than this. "If you see me again, I need it to be because I chose this, okay?" I said, knowing full well she'd likely not be able to understand.

The glimmer in her eyes dulled, and I watched as her expression shifted through what felt like a thousand emotions. The one that settled was harsh and full of outrage. She took a threatening step toward me, reaching for my hands as I shot them into my pockets. My knuckles hit something hard and rigid. I pulled it out for a quick glance—the fucking crystal. Of course. "Get my ass out of here," I said, holding it tight.

Mother screamed as I shot away from her, whizzing past stars and plunging through clouds until I was violently dropped back into the safety of my living room. I hit the floor and my head spun for...I don't know how long...but once I managed to move just enough to see my house hadn't actually been blown to smithereens, I sobbed into my new carpet.

After a few days off work to recover, I walked with a bit more pep in my step to Sadie's desk. "Found the crystal," I said. She turned around and smiled as I held it up, confirming I found the exact one she'd given me. "And, if you ever have another one of those parties, I think I'd like to come. If you'll have me."

She smiled, offering an aggressively white set of perfect teeth, and I allowed her a solid four to five minutes of gloating responses before bolting back to my desk.

Merry Go

Maria Brekke

Maria is an attorney who writes short stories in various genres and is working on a fantasy novel. She has taken courses and workshops with the Loft Literary Center and Sackett Street Writers. "Beech, Please," in the December 2022 edition of Luna Station Quarterly, is her first fiction publication. Maria lives in Minnesota, USA, with her husband, daughter, and dog.

Merry rose and fell to the music as she had for a hundred years, keeping her painted eyes on the mat of brown hair in front of her. When Royal gave the signal, she was going to steal that toupée.

On her next ascent, she caught Royal's eye through the mirror that lined the carousel's interior. He winked and shrugged his shoulders forward in anticipation, his silver reins reflecting the fairy lights. In front of Merry, Lyle shook on his pole. He was the calmest of the forty-eight horses, which is why they'd so carefully orchestrated the boarding process to mount their target on his back, but Merry worried even Lyle wouldn't let Gerard McFadden slosh wine down his flank.

"This was my first carousel," Gerard boasted to the woman on the horse beside him. "A bit shabby compared to my newer models," he added, kicking Lyle in the side, "but it brings me a particular satisfaction."

Gerard had always been arrogant and strong, a combination that empowered him to open doors better left closed. Merry and the caravan of enchanters who'd taken in two orphaned siblings— the people who loved him—tried to drag Gerard back from the threshold, but he was already drunk on the dark divinity within.

He cursed his sister and their found family, transforming them into a twisted carnival ride.

"Your carousels are a wonder, Mr. President," the woman replied, her voice an octave higher than it should have been.

"They are certainly a luxury," Gerard said with a gracious nod, "but I think I've earned a few creature comforts after all the rebuilding I have done."

Merry craned her neck, waiting, waiting for the moment when she could tear the crown off her brother's head and untether the power beneath his hair, restoring it to its rightful owners.

The organ shifted keys, playing another song in a repertoire Merry hoped she would never have to hear again. Usually, her riders were screeching children throwing popcorn. Tonight, Gerard had brought the country's luminaries to commemorate his hundred-year reign, and his guests had adorned themselves with enough gems to fill a museum. Horses began quietly nipping bracelets off arms and diamonds from rings and watches. No stone was too small. For years they'd practiced, learning how to use the specks of magic Gerard hadn't stolen to enchant motion into their limbs, taking beads from shoelaces or ripping wristbands with their teeth. Merry, still as a statue, focused on the toupée in front of her.

The organ launched into another tune, and Royal brayed. Riders screamed at the hideous sound, and one man dropped his glass. It was time.

Across the carousel, Doreen kicked the light switch. The lights spluttered, leaving the carousel in darkness—and cutting off Gerard's power source.

The woman next to Gerard shrieked.

"Not to worry, my dear," he said, his voice echoing around the circle. "The power must have gone out."

The carousel glided on, the music eerier without the twinkling lights and smiling faces. Merry had one revolution of the carousel to grab the toupée. She began counting down. The other horses nudged the jewelry into a pattern around the floorboards, ignoring the screams and hisses of their riders.

20...19...18.

"But we're still spinning," the woman was saying. "Why are we still spinning?"

Merry inched her neck forward. She had to time it just right, when Lyle was at his lowest point and she was halfway up again. It was almost impossible in the dark, but luckily, Merry had been staring at Lyle's ugly backside for a century. 10...9...8.

Snap! Merry grabbed the toupéefrom Gerard's head. Gerard roared, flailing toward Merry, but Lyle craned back and bit his jacket. The horses on either side of Lyle snaked their reins around Gerard's arms and wrenched them outward, immobilizing him.

3...2...1.

Doreen hit the switch again. The lights came back, brighter after the darkness. Perfectly positioned around the carousel, dozens of gems were arranged to reflect the lights at Gerard's gleaming bald head. The source of all his magic, and it was theirs to harness.

The horses began to whinny their spell, harmonizing with the lush music. The gems pulsed with light as the spell pulled out their energy, funneling it through Gerard's head, which glowed like the sun itself. Merry's rider whimpered.

But then Gerard started chanting, his harsh baritone clashing with the horses' melody and choking their spell. *His mouth is free*, Merry realized. *Something must have gone wrong.* Remy, the horse in front of Lyle, was supposed to gag Gerard. Merry craned around Lyle and saw Remy's predicament: his rider was clinging to his head, suffocating him with her fear.

Merry still had a mouthful of toupée. Could she somehow disarm Gerard? Her mind raced as the carousel spun, the lights flickering with the unstable magic of the two dueling spells.

Pop! A bulb exploded above Merry, showering her in sparks and glass. Merry's rider screamed and scraped her hands down Merry's flank, reminding Merry of sticky fingers groping her wooden body. *That's it.* Some of the things those sticky hands had deposited were still there. Merry used her reins to pull the gum off her belly, frantically sticking it inside the toupée.

Pop–pop-pop! Lights were burning out all around her. Time was running out.

She brayed at Lyle through the hair, and he met her gaze in the mirror. Letting go of Gerard's jacket, he kicked outward and spun on his pole to face her. Gerard's arms crossed as the reins pulled even tighter, and his chanting faltered when he saw Merry. She tossed the toupéeat him. It started to fall, slouching down his face—then the gum stuck. Gerard's mouth disappeared behind a mound of shaggy hair, silenced.

The horses whinnied louder. Gerard's bald crown glowed brighter. When Merry couldn't stand the light another second, every remaining bulb shattered in a synchronized explosion. The horses glided to a stop, and the organ went quiet.

At first, nothing happened. Merry waited, inhaling the darkness like a prayer.

The pole through Merry's back began to twist, braided gold spinning upward. Around her, horses brayed. Royal reared and bucked his rider. For the first time in a century, he lunged forward, breaking free from the worn path.

Forty-six enchanters followed him, shedding their horse-forms as they stepped off the carousel. Merry alone hesitated. Gerard knelt on the ground, pulling at the toupée, but it had spread, covering his body in a thick layer of fur. His power was no more. Merry huffed and nudged him onto all fours on the carousel track. Then she leapt into the starry night.

The Last Ride of Rivke Grinkin

Reyzl Grace

Reyzl Grace is a poet, essayist, translator, short story writer, and post-Soviet Jewish lesbian from Alaska. Her work has been nominated for the Pushcart Prize, named a finalist for the Jewish Women's Poetry Prize and Best Literary Translations, and featured in Room, Rust & Moth, the Times of Israel, and elsewhere. By day, she is a teen services librarian in Minneapolis—by night, a poetry editor for Psaltery & Lyre and Cordella Magazine. You can find more of her at reyzlgrace.com and on Twitter/ Bluesky @reyzlgrace.

In the thirty-fourth cavalry regiment, there was some discussion whether Komot Rivke Grinkin or her horse was the more disciplined soldier. In truth, Rivke wasn't sure herself, but if she'd had a kopek to spare, she would have bet it on Dvora, who had kept her alive at Bataisk and brought her through Egorlykskaia.

Even here, at full gallop across a Polish field with a rain of mortars to either side, she feared nothing so long as Dvora's hooves were under her. Had the corner of her eye not caught the two left hooves rising like a pair of slow moons over the flank of the Russian Don, she might well have gone on fearlessly, straight through the young woman who apparated in front of them as though born from a glint of sun off a horseshoe.

But her eye *had* caught them, along with a spray of dirt from the ground her horse was being swept off of, and she flinched, twisting the reins tighter around white knuckles. When she opened her eyes again, she was still being carried forward by the inertia of twelve hundred pounds of airborne mare, but the rotation of the earth seemed to have slowed, as though matching the patience of the young woman, who grew neither larger nor more alarmed as she browsed the head of the horse that should have been colliding with her, examining every detail as though she were deciding whether to buy it, though she did not look at all like someone in the habit of doing her own horse trading.

Masses of platinum hair spilled over epaulettes, and rivers of Austrian knots flooded the sleeves of a sumptuous vermilion riding coat, its every detail as exactly tailored as its wearer's cheekbones. For a soldier who had run Denikin's men to ground, she recalled the mist that draped the Caucasus on dawn patrol. To a peasant from Zaporizhzhia, she looked like a Romanov princess at riding lessons.

"Who...*are* you?" Rivke whispered, almost to herself.

The young woman's pale blue eyes flashed like flame from the mouth of a cannon, and she snapped them from the horse to its rider. Her head tilted. "You can see me?"

Rivke's brown eyes widened to match. "*You* speak *Yiddish*, blondie?"

"I speak whatever you need me to," the young woman smiled.

It was hard to reconcile the perfectly normal movement of her lips with the slow flail of Dvora's hooves as the horse's panicked body rotated languidly through open air, like a dancer in a music box coming to the end of its wind. The horizon was moving too, creeping leftward like a minute hand run in reverse. For the moment, it was still shy of vertical, but close enough to be disorienting as puffs of dirt and grass flew with all the gentle leisure of drifting dandelion seeds from right to left with every landed bullet. Over Rivke's head, another horse swept with the dynamism of an airplane but the speed of a slow cloud, its head and hooves stretched wide from one end of her vision to the other. Its rider was another of the squad leaders, who spoke like he came from Kharkiv. She couldn't remember his name.

Rivke's mind swam—in possibilities, in folk tales, in Yiddish and Ukrainian and Russian, in that shining hair, in cool mountain lakes where she used to go skinny dipping, in sloshed cerebral fluid rapidly growing shallow against one side of her skull. "Are you . . ." but before she could find the words, the wind off a second nearby shell swept between them, and the young woman, trying to brush the hair out of her face, looked down.

"A *woman!*?" she gasped, picking up fistfuls of curls only to let them drop against her chest again and again. "Yes—yes, I am! This has never happened before! Look!" Rivke watched, awkwardly mesmerized, as the stranger carefully felt out the contours of her jacket with both hands. Ages seemed to pass before the young woman looked up again with moist eyes and a tremble tugging at a plump lip. Her voice was suddenly very quiet. "I always wanted to be a woman. No one has ever imagined me this way."

Rivke's eyes felt dry but she couldn't blink. "What? No! Are you . . ." again she struggled for the words, ". . . here for *me?*" It all sounded strange coming out; she was sure the words were what she meant to say, but she wasn't at all sure what they were trying to ask.

"Oh! No, dear." The young woman said this very simply, but her face grew somber, even as one hand continued to pat obsessively between her waist and her hip. "I'm here for the horse."

This phrase ricocheted off Rivke slowly. "For the horse?"

"Yes." The young woman's nod was earnest. "I like horses. The Name lets me see to them." She returned her attention to Rivke's mount. "Does your horse have a name?"

Rivke felt like she'd just come up out of a lake with ears still full of water, someone on the shore waving and yelling something she couldn't make out. "Yes. I mean, it's Dvora."

"Of *course* it is!" cooed the young woman, admiring the shine of the Don's golden chestnut coat. She repeated softly, as though to herself this time, "Of course it is. She would have liked this horse, too."

At that moment, the shockwave that had called attention to the young woman's hair caught up with the horse that was, from Rivke's perspective, running on its side overhead, sweeping it suddenly straight up out of her field of vision, as though it and its rider had been taken by Elijah. The nameless man from Kharkiv was gone, but this didn't seem to trouble the young woman in the least.

Gently, she patted Dvora's wet nose and whispered in her ear, while Rivke watched in astonishment as the distressed animal settled under the touch of the young woman's painted nails, which gleamed like little revolutionary banners snapped taut against peach-colored clouds at sunset, but with their yellow stars and sickles replaced by impossibly fine gold-leaf knotwork. Something about the design against the backdrop of Dvora's head stirred Rivke's memory; it seemed like something she might have seen when she was young—like some bit of old Rus gold-work in a Kyiv museum.

The horizon continued to shift slowly, sky giving way to earth as the torn mud and grass of the field expanded leftward, rising to meet her in a lancework of shrapnel and stone. What remained of sky was silence, thick over everything she could see, so that the only sound was the phrase ringing in her head—*I'm here for the horse.*

Every soldier knows the day may come and gives some thought

to what they might say when it does. And in this moment, Rivke Grinkin—champion sharpshooter of the Sixth Division, terror of the Whites, daughter of Abraham and Job and Habakkuk—drew herself together to tell fate what she truly thought of it.

"I, uh...I like horses, too."

The young woman's eyes shone and her voice soared. "Aren't they *incredible?*" she gushed, gesticulating eagerly over the whole length of the lofted animal. "Such powerful creatures, like a rising constellation remade in flesh! And yet so effortlessly graceful—slender as the limits of bone and muscle will allow. And then," she brought her distant hand back in toward the horse's head, "it all comes to its zenith here, and you can see in their eyes, even when you don't feel it on your hand," she chuckled as Dvora's lips smacked against her palm, taking a treat that seemed to have come from nowhere, "how deeply *gentle* they are at the very core of their being." Her eyes moved from Rivke back to her mount as she stroked behind the horse's ears. "Speed and strength that make legends"—the words were almost a lullaby—"and asymptotic tenderness. They're like angels..."

"It's even better when you ride them!" blurted Rivke. "They experience everything so differently than we do—so much more directly." Her courage flooded back to her, and for a moment she forgot she was on a horse headed into the ground—could imagine herself on the ground getting ready to climb in the saddle. "When I started riding, I thought of the horse like a partner; I tried to talk to them—communicate with them like I would a person. But then I realized that's not how horses do things! To Dvora, I'm not another horse in a herd—I'm *a part of her*; she treats me like an extension of her own body. I don't give her commands any more than my lips give me commands when the coffee's too hot; there's just a *knowing* that flows through us both when I get my damned head out of the way and let myself *know* in the hands that are on the reins, in the feet that are in the stirrups . . ."

Rivke searched for the words for something more, but she could feel Dvora's back quiver, her anxiety rising, and she realized that the young woman's hands had left the horse. They were cupped, instead, under her gently cleft chin, red-nailed fingers clapped to rosy cheeks as she hung, rapt and waiting, on Rivke's next word. When it didn't come, she simply sighed, "That's amazing!"

Rivke fumbled for another thought that could meet the expectation. "Um...do you ride?"

"Not like you do. How did you learn? Tell me about your first horse!"

"Oh, Persik? I actually never got to ride her. I grew up on a farm, and, when I was five or six, my father gave me one of the old mares as mine to look after. I fed her and brushed her every day and *begged* to ride, but my mother said I needed to wait until I was a little older. But Persik was old already, and the next year she broke her ankle, and my father took her out behind the old barn and shot her." Rivke's eyes were far away—far past the waning slice of sky on the left side of her vision. "That's the terrible thing about this war, you know. My father will wave a red banner if it means he gets to shoot a Cossack, but he shot a loyal worker just as easily when she wasn't useful to him. To a horse, all of us are kulaks. And if that's how we treat animals, what makes us think we'll treat people any better?"

The young woman still had her eyes locked on Rivke, but they had grown sad. "Why fight, then?"

"It's a chance to live until I don't. What's the alternative? Let the shadkhnte have her way with me—give me over to be ridden by a man who...who doesn't understand the intelligence of my body?" Dvora was flailing again, but Rivke was atypically at ease, although the young woman hadn't touched her. *The young woman*...All in a moment, Rivke's focus returned to the foreground, and she remembered whom she was talking to. Her eyes scanned the curious face for any hint of condemnation, but found none. The waiting was unbearable, swelling like a blister on her brain until she had to lance it.

"They serve pork in the mess tent," she said suddenly.

A smile pulled at the young woman's lips, but she held her face steady. "I figured."

"And I eat it," Rivke added, emphasizing the word *eat* in a note of defiance.

"You have to eat something." Heaps of curls slid from the young woman's shoulders as she shrugged. Rivke's mouth opened again but the young woman cut her off. "Let me guess, you missed shul last Yom Kippur."

"Not what I was going to say, but yes."

The young woman nodded matter-of-factly, her voice level and kind. "We all do what we have to. You said it yourself—it's a chance to live. Pikuakh nefesh. That's not why I'm just here for Dvora."

Rivke's eye was steady, but her voice was uneven. "And I'm glad. I always thought that, when all this is done, she will be free. I've been saving some pay to buy land—to take her far from here. Somewhere out east. Maybe Tajikistan. And when we get there, I'll hop down from her back and let the bridle fall, and I won't tie her up or put her in the barn or anything. And then, if she stays with me anyway, I'll know we'll be together for life."

The young woman pressed her lips, and Rivke felt the pressure in her chest. "I'm impressed the two of you are together now," she said. "You're a fine rider; not many people would still be in that saddle." She looked back at Dvora, took the horse's head in her hands again and calmed it as she added, "Though even you won't be, in a moment."

At the edge of Rivke's vision, all four hooves were now cantilevered above the level of her shoulder. Her breathing grew shallow, but that could have been coincidence. "Horses are *all* you do?" she confirmed. "All the time? I mean, surely you like other things, too?"

The young woman's cheeks flushed the color of her coat, and she busied herself harder in smoothing the muzzle. "Ah . . ." she chuckled. "Um, well...There was this one time . . ." Her blue eyes flicked up like the tail of a mischievous horse before becoming buried in Dvora's coat again, leaving Rivke with an inexplicable tickle on the end of her nose. "I mean, the Name just has me care for horses now."

In Rivke's eyes, ground had all but occluded sky, and the young woman was the only thing that didn't grow darker. "Do *you* have a name?"

The young woman looked up at her again, and for a second time her eyes glistened with tears in the corners. "You want to know my name? Now?" Her glances flitted around Dvora's tack as though she might find it written on a label somewhere, but finally settled again on Rivke's face. "You can call me Tsariel."

To a girl from the Pale who spoke no Hebrew, this sounded grander than it was, and Rivke played with the sound of it under her breath for a little while, until it dawned on her that she couldn't hear it. Bullets struck the earth but did not whistle. Men were unhorsed but did not scream. The world ran like a film, as though stunned into silence by Tsariel's perfect serenity.

"I can't hear anything but you," she confessed, and once again she wasn't sure what she was really trying to say.

Tsariel nodded sadly. "You're deaf—bleeding out both ears, actually. You just haven't noticed the trickles yet."

"Then how can I hear you?"

"That's not how I talk to you."

"Then why are your lips moving?"

"Because people are disquieted when they don't. But you understand what that's like—going through the motions so as not to alarm folk."

"What do you mean?"

Tsariel took a thick lock of blonde hair between her fingers, and a sly smile winked at the corner of her lip. "You like Russian girls," she teased. "What would your mother say?"

"Does it matter?" asked Rivke. "It's not like I'll ever get to bring one home, anyway."

"Well, that's the point, isn't it?"

Tsariel's words hung in the air between them for a long moment before Rivke repeated herself. "What do you mean?"

The blonde bit thoughtfully at a knuckle. Her eyes grew more intense. "Do you think you could want me to be different?"

"Different how?"

"I appear as you want me to appear. Do you think you could want my hair to be darker, my face a little longer, for there to be a little more color in my hands? How have you imagined Miriam when she was young? Or Rachel at the well?"

Rivke looked at her, and Tsariel seemed just a little less solid than before. "I think," she said slowly, "that I could want you to be anything you would like to be."

Suddenly, the young woman to whom neither horse nor rider ever seemed to get any closer stood face-to-face with Rivke. The Romanov princess was gone, and in her place stood a girl from the shtetl—the prettiest girl in the shtetl, to be sure, but a girl from the shtetl all the same—with masses of russet hair curling into fine-cut cheeks that glowed as Tsariel surveyed her new arms and again drew out locks of hair in her fingers to admire. Several times, she looked as though she wanted to say something, but no sound came out, and Rivke wondered if her companion was simply overcome or if she had gone deaf in a new and deeper way looking at her. But at last, the words came through. "Thank you." She was close enough now for Rivke to feel her breath on her face. "Thank you. It's perfect! No. It's more than perfect..." Tsariel's eyes came up off her hair to meet Rivke's. "It's the closest I've ever been to being free."

Rivke's own breath was heavy, and she didn't know if it was because the ground was so close or this girl was. "I think," she said, and her voice was small even as her heart swelled, "that this is the nearest I've come to being alive."

Rivke closed her eyes, and, though her face was now fully in Dvora's shadow, the feeling on her lips was like the warmth of the sun on a winter day, ethereal and tangible at the same time, bleeding into every part of her body. On the other side of her eyelids, Tsariel's hand shot at the bridle, only for her elbow to lock preternaturally short of grasping the leather. Unseen, her lips were again formless—able, simultaneously, to hold the kiss, be bitten through, and form a litany of curses around the words "so close" in a thousand languages.

Rivke sighed.

The horse came down.

Hospitality

Jennifer Skogen

Jennifer Skogen is the author of The Haunting of Grey Hills young adult series, and her work has been featured in journals including Lady Churchill's Rosebud Wristlet, Green Ink Poetry, Bowery Gothic, Tales from the Moonlit Path, and FERAL. Jennifer lives near Seattle, Washington, and goes hiking in beautiful places whenever it isn't raining.

The young man was gone. Caroline stood in her parents' barn, feeling foolish as the freshly baked bread that was supposed to be his breakfast grew cold in her hands. It was still dark outside, and she didn't like to think of him climbing that narrow mountain path without at least having something warm to eat. Without morning light to guide his way.

A chill wind brushed along her bare neck, and up the sleeves of her dress. She could no longer deny the approach of winter. At least snow would mean fewer visitors.

Over breakfast no one mentioned the young man, Frederick, who only last night had shared their dinner and told them stories about his home by the sea. He had traveled weeks to come to the mountain, and Caroline swore she could smell salt wind on his clothes. Usually, she didn't bother to remember names, but she'd liked his. *Frederick.* She thought it sounded like rolling a sharp rock in your mouth.

Her parents hadn't tried to warn him away from the wild mountain horses – their predator's teeth and silent wings. They only mentioned how cold it was up there, where winter had already arrived. *Had he brought enough clothes? Did he know how to build a fire?* Then they'd all chatted cheerfully about the autumn market in town, and asked if he'd seen any of the traders on his journey east. Her father kept a small dairy, and wanted to know if the young man had ever tasted such fine cheese. Frederick was full of compliments: the sweet, creamy cheese was excellent, and the thick beef stew her mother made was sure to send him to bed with warm dreams. How amazed Frederick was, to find such rich, fine food offered to a guest, so late in the season. Such hospitality.

No one mentioned the other young men who had ventured to the mountain before him.

He insisted they take a stack of coins, though her parents protested. They always protested at first, wanting to appear – perhaps even to themselves – that they housed the young men out of the generosity owed weary travelers. But those coins had helped her father buy some of his best milk cows, and had paid for Caroline's fine winter boots.

If their family were to lay their ledgers bare, it would show that over the years those coins from foolhardy young men had brought in more money each year than the dairy ever could. The young men were always loose with their money when they spent their last night in the village, for they must have known they would either have no further need for coin where they were going, or they would come home wealthy beyond imagining.

Recently, Caroline had noticed that the men who stayed with them were growing younger and younger. Frederick had seemed to shrink into his chair as he sat down to dinner. She'd wanted to pat his head and tuck him into bed that night with a warm glass of milk, though he was older than her by at least a handful of years. She supposed, reluctantly, that it was because she had grown up—soon she would have to give one of the village boys an answer and be done with it. Even Caroline knew that a woman could not continue unattached at her age unless she wanted to draw scandal. Women were not like these young men, able to follow wherever their shadows led them on a sunny day.

All that morning, after he had gone up the mountain, Caroline thought about Frederick's wide brown eyes, and how he ducked his head when complimenting her mother. He hadn't seemed like so many of the other men who chased horses. They were loud, crass, and talked enthusiastically about how straight they could shoot an arrow. How adept their tracking skills. More than one of those men had extended a hand to Caroline when the dinner candles were growing low and he thought her parents might not see. But her parents always saw. That was why the guest room was so often kept empty, and the visitors slept in the barn.

And Frederick hadn't seemed like the village boys, either. They were always smirking at her like she belonged to them already, and it was just a matter of deciding which one. Yes, it was *her* choice, but a choice of which apple to pick from the same tree, no matter if they were all worm-eaten.

Frederick hadn't been loud, or crass, and he'd smiled in a friendly, not leering, way when Caroline and her mother had shown him to the barn and bid him goodnight. He could have stayed in the guestroom, she thought as she went about her chores, mucking stalls and hauling water. He could have slept in a bed instead of making do with a few blankets and a pile of hay. But he was gone just the same, so she supposed that it didn't matter how he had spent his last night.

It didn't matter, either, that when he had smiled at her by candlelight, she couldn't help smiling back, couldn't help the warmth that kindled her cheeks and deep in her stomach – an ember that burned hours later as she lay in bed trying to sleep, planning how early she could bring him breakfast the next morning. Planning exactly how she would tell him goodbye.

No, none of that mattered. The young men who hunted the winged horses were not meant for her. Once they started on their journey, they belonged only to the mountain.

Caroline wondered at these young men who kept coming to her doorstep, their eyes always sweeping up towards the hazy gray and green contours of the mountain. Was it bravery that led them up the trail? Ignorance? Greed? Surely, they realized that ninety-nine out of a hundred of their brethren never returned. Surely, they must have known they were throwing their lives to the wind...But they seemed to only consider the one man out of a hundred who did return. The one lucky hunter who came home victorious.

Once when she was ten years old, and then again when she was twelve, she had seen men return with tawny wings wrapped in a cloak, blood from the severed stumps seeping into the fabric. She'd wept when she saw the wings, shown off like a prize by those radiant, triumphant men. She'd wanted to scream at them, ask if they realized what they'd done. If they knew what they had killed when they struck down those wondrous horses.

Her parents had taken her aside the first time a young man returned and explained that this was the way of it. Sometimes the mountain took the men, and sometimes—much rarer—the men took something back from the mountain. The hunters had to win sometimes, or they would not return. Their coins would not feed the village as they purchased supplies and drank ale for courage, and stayed the night in houses like theirs. So yes, sometimes the men needed to win what they were seeking. Sometimes they needed an arrow to strike the thick vein of a horse's neck, and surely the mountain knew it, too.

When the men did bring home a horse, they only ever took the wings. They left the rest to rot high up on the mountain, for how would they have carried anything more home? They could not bring their own hooved horses or donkeys up the trail. The feathers from the horse's wings were long and sharp, and the same warm brown as a hawk's feather—mottled for the sun-dappled forest of the high reaches. Such feathers were worn by lords and ladies as adornments for their hair and dresses, and legend said that when dipped in blood they could write the future. There were other legends, too. Caroline had heard that a king was murdered by his jealous mistress when she stabbed a feather through his eye. But no one ever said which king, or which year.

Another tale spoke of a hunter who had gone mad while on the mountain. When he returned with his bloody bundle and spread it before the high lords and ladies, expecting to have riches heaped upon him, all he revealed from beneath the cloak was a pair of severed arms. The story ended with this hunter being strung up and executed as a murderer, for the arms had belonged to the land's own missing prince—evidenced by a signet ring still glinting from one of the dead fingers.

Caroline didn't know if any of the stories were true, or if the only thing the feathers ever bestowed upon those rich enough to buy them was beauty. The only truth she knew was that most of the men never came back from the mountain.

More than once, Caroline thought she had heard distant voices: shrieks that ended suddenly, leaving only the wind. Many people assumed it was wild cats, or the cold, or the horses themselves that had gotten them. Or they had simply walked off the side of a cliff. All of these were likely true in their way – so many of the hunters were ill-prepared for the realities of the mountain. Men's bones had been found, on occasion, scattered below sheer cliff-faces, spread by animals far from the rise of the mountain itself.

Her parents didn't like to speak of what they thought happened to the men. There were things you simply didn't talk about – things you just did because you had to. Perhaps it was that way for the young men, too...Perhaps something drew them to the horses, a call beyond their power to resist. Other legends spoke of a wild woman, a witch who lived up in the mountain and kept the winged horses as her pets. A woman who haunted the ridge-line, who drank the blood of eagles and bathed in alpenglow. A woman who belonged only to herself. The legend said that she protected her horses, and that was why so few men ever returned successful from the hunt.

Caroline had never seen such a woman – not when she stared up at the mountain, and not in her own village. She didn't think such a woman could exist.

Another thing Caroline and her parents didn't tell the young men was that they had seen the mountain horses for themselves. Winters were harsh in their village, and blizzards could last for days. Sometimes, when a snow flurry blinded even the sharpest eyes, one of the winged horses would find its way down the mountain. Perhaps the horses were turned around in the snow. Perhaps something else drew them to their farm – the smell of a woodfire, or the lights glowing in their snowy windows. Whenever her family found one of the mountain horses roaming outside their house, Caroline and her parents would shoo it into the barn and keep it locked up until the weather cleared and the horse could find its way back up to the high cliffs. They always let the horses go free – they only ever offered them shelter until the weather cleared. Never would her parents, or anyone in the village, consider harming what the mountain owned.

They never told any of the men about those winter nights. Or that sometimes, if the storm did not cease in a day or so, they would push one of the young cows inside the barn. Caroline didn't like to think about the sounds, or how there was never any blood left over after the sun came out and they let the horse go.

Just bones, as clean as the snow.

A few days later snow fell deep, in huge, wet flakes that always seemed about to turn to rain. Caroline put on her tall, warm boots and a thick cloak, and went out to break ice from her favorite calf's water trough and feed him a handful of sweet barley. The calf was getting big. Soon her father would decide if he would be kept for breeding stock or sold in the spring. He had a gray face and thick lashes, and his wide nose pushed against her palm even when all the grain was gone. Always wanting more than she offered.

Just as she raised a branch to crack the thin sheet of snowy ice, she felt something warm huff against the back of her head. Turning, she kept the branch raised. There stood a horse, blinking snow from his huge brown eyes.

"You came back," Caroline whispered, lowering the branch. The horse bared his sharp teeth; his breath was warm and thick, and smelled of salt. He stretched out his wings, and snow clung to the beautiful, tawny feathers.

Leading him to the barn, Caroline was almost certain his plumed ears swiveled in recognition when she spoke his name.

Rain Town

Mary J. Daley

Mary J. Daley lives with her spouse in Atlantic Canada, where she currently divides her time between writing and barn chores. Her publishing credits include On Spec, Kaleidotrope, Triangulation, Every Day Fiction and others.

His heavy black coat held onto the rain. Not a drop dripped from its hem. His horse, a shade wetter, stood behind him, head lowered. Every one of its ribs an acknowledgement to the Drylands they had come through.

"We don't get many showing up here anymore." Pop held his rifle lax by his side, as if trying not to appear menacing. "If you're looking for citizenship, you'll have to see the mayor four houses down." He swung the gun point in that direction. "Apple tree out front."

"I'm only looking to stay a few weeks. To put a little weight on the horse before moving on," the man said.

Pop just stood there, as if not quite comprehending. "Moving on? The direction you just come from is all the direction there is now."

Ma came out onto the porch then, a dish towel in her hands. "Gael, how long you plan on leaving that man in the rain? Bring him in, let him get into something dry. Looks like a proper meal couldn't hurt him either." She gave me a bit of a shove, inching me out from under the porch roof and into the downpour. "And Lyn, take his horse around back. Give him some hay. Just a little. We don't want to shock the poor thing."

"He'd appreciate that." The tall man smiled down at me as he removed the saddlebags. I took the reins and led the horse around back and into the dry barn. Jenny, our piebald mare, nickered.

The saddle was light as I pulled it from the horse. Well-made, its leather supple, not a stitch to be found, but the horse was still significantly chafed across the withers. So much so, that when the lamplight caught a glint of shine, I took it as bone. I was wrong. It was steel. Excitedly, I lifted a front hoof to inspect.

***

When I returned to the house, the man's coat and hat hung near the stove. He sat at the kitchen table. A plate of corn rice in front of him and a glass of my pop's holiday whisky in his hand. Ma and Pop sat across from him.

"This here is Reyen," My pop introduced him.

I nodded a welcome. "He has a gaming horse, Pop. Like Mayor Atkens."

Pop glanced at me before returning to Reyen. "Never thought a gaming horse could look as worn as an organic. Nothing chased you here, did it?"

Reyen shook his head. "Unless I'm to count the dart birds and the odd guanas?"

"Nah, we don't worry about them much. They aren't partial to rain. Not that we don't lose the occasional sheep, and even a dog to them sometimes, in the fields along the edges."

Ma stood and smoothed out her skirt. "The mayor will want to know that you're here. It wouldn't do to keep it from him too long."

Reyen pushed away from the table. It looked to take some effort.

"No, sit and finish your meal," Ma said. "You can make his acquaintance when you're rested. I'll go let him know you'll be staying with us."

"Best not to mention the horse, Tarry," Pop said to her.

Ma put on her jacket. "But if he asks where you originate from, where might I say?"

"Crowdown."

Pop sat a little straighter. Ma paused with her hand on the doorknob, as if wanting to sit back down to hear more, but the task at hand won and she entered the rain.

"Impossible. How'd you come through the dust up there?" Pop asked.

Reyen stared down into his drink. "Dust was all but dead for a stretch along our section for three years straight. Not a stir. We got to thinking it wouldn't rise again. A few of us took that chance and headed across to Tabletop, to one of the bigger gaming domes, to see what we could salvage. We found ourselves a treasure trove. All as pristine as the day they built it. We made three trips over the course of that year, hauling what we could back to Crowdown. The energy cells alone were a Godsend. But the dust started up on our last return, and we found ourselves trapped on this side of it. We went west for a considerable distance but found no break in it. So, we headed south."

"And the others with you?"

"Dead. All except Anton, who stayed on in Lawrenceville."

"And you continued on because?" Pop continued to press.

"Because I aim to get back to my family and I don't like the possibility that the dust might take another twenty years to set-tle. I plan to go around it."

Pop leaned in. Not just curious anymore. He appeared hope-ful. "How?"

"By crossing Titan's Trench." Reyen put down his glass and pulled a map from the saddlebag that was resting at the foot of his chair. He took his time unfolding the map and placing it on the table. His finger came down hard twice on a spot much south of us where the trench narrowed considerably. "I'm hoping there's still a bridge at Greendale. If not, I'll rebuild it. Once over, I'll head north again."

I stepped closer to follow his finger along the ever-widening trench until it rounded the far northern end and came down this side again to the town of Crowdown.

"There's little dust now on that side of the trench, is what I heard," Reyen said.

"Not much of nothing over there now," Pop said. "And even if that bridge remains, you're all out of rain towns."

"What about Reference Point?"

"Dried up."

"Radium?"

"Not entirely sure, since no one can reach it now that Reference Point is gone. But my guess it's gone too. Like I was saying, no one comes from that direction anymore."

Reyen was quiet for a moment. "Still aim to try. This Mayor of yours. How partial is he to his gaming horse? I have a few items from Tabletop he might find a fair trade."

"He won't part with it. It wins the Harvest Day race every year," I blurt.

Pop chuckled. "True. Although, it's akin to giving the yearly purse to the mechanical rabbit at a dog race, but there's nothing in the rule book that says he can't enter it since it got some organic in it. It was one of a set of four that belonged to the carriage service up in Wet Cross that routinely passed through here at one time."

I nodded and urged Pop to continue with the story. "Tell him how April Brown and Bell Thompson stole the horses and carriage, and set off East, and how Charger showed up here a year later."

"Mayor Atkens found the horse standing forlorn with his sheep," Pop added. "Almost a year after the incident. Around the same time Wet Cross, itself, went dry. And ever since, our mayor has been winning the Harvest Day race every damn year. It's why I told Tarry not to tell him what type of horse you came in on. He'll only figure out a way to take it off you. He doesn't have to know you have anything else of value on your person either. Understand?'

Reyen sat quietly for a few minutes before finally starting in on the corn rice.

***

I could tell straight off Reyen didn't like Mayor Atkens. He held himself stiff when the mayor entered our house an hour later. Larry Bain and Martin Che, who always accompanied the mayor, remained outside, under the porch roof. Larry had his rifle with him, resting the barrel on his shoulder. The mayor was tall and wide and took up much of the entrance as he removed his hat and shook the rain from it, not minding that he splashed

Ma as he tossed it to her. He did the same with his yellow jacket. He then grabbed my father's hand in his wet one, while his deep voice filled the parts of the room that his physicality couldn't reach.

"How you keeping, Gael? When your pretty wife showed up at my door, I figured she might have finally come looking for someone a little more substantial." He laughed and slapped a large hand down on Pop's shoulder while still gripping his hand. He then helped himself to a glass of the whisky before stepping over to the stove to examine Reyen's coat.

"Tarry asked if I'd wait until tomorrow to stop by, but I thought, shit, someone claiming they're from up north, This I have to check out." He turned and finally acknowledged Reyen. "Crowdown, you say?"

Reyen nodded politely.

"We'll just have to take your word on that for now," the mayor said. "I see you're already making yourself pretty comfortable."

"We're fine with putting him up," Pop said.

The mayor raised his hand. "I know. You're good folk but we have barracks set up for this sort of thing."

"Reyen's more than welcome to stay in our spare room if he prefers," Ma said, still holding the mayor's wet jacket and hat.

"If you feel the need to be hospitable, that's up to you. But he's still got to contribute. We'll put him on irrigation starting tomorrow," the mayor said.

Ma laughed. "You can't be serious. He's worn through. Give him a few days to right himself." Ma was twisting the mayor's hat now, possibly regretting fetching him.

"That's fine. A night's sleep is all I need. If I can earn my keep, I'll feel better about imposing," Reyen said, although his eyes seemed to shade some as he watched the mayor search his coat's pockets.

"Good. We like team players here, don't we Lyn?"

I was caught off guard by the mayor's rare acknowledgement of me, and I reluctantly turned to face him, nodding.

***

The horse put on weight. So did Reyen, even though he spent long hours of each day keeping the irrigation ditches clear. Ma made sure his breakfast was always substantial and his lunchbox full. For the most part, he hid his exhaustion from us, although he did retire to his room almost immediately following every evening meal.

Sometimes Pop would ask to borrow his map, and the three of us would sit and study it under the lamplight. Not that we didn't have our own map of the territories, but Reyen's gave us a newer, sadder version. There were several towns up north that were crossed out. Lake Head and Lake Heart were marked dry. These deep lakes once teemed with fish and took a person weeks to ride around. The only positive addition to the map was an apparent stretch of grassland located just south of Parton, where Reyen had scribbled in an almost illegible hand 'miles of meadow and yellow flower. Rains in intervals here.' He had also marked the places where he had spotted guanas or worst creatures. It was astonishing he got this far. It was more astonishing that he was preparing to keep going.

***

One evening, at mealtime, just before Reyen disappeared into the back room to change into something drier, he paused and asked, "What can you tell me about McClusky?"

Ma glanced at Pop.

"Do they have him working on irrigation with you?" Pop asked.

Reyen shook his head. "But I am working along his property. I guess I'm just curious what happened to it."

"A string of bad luck, beginning with his main ditch collapsing, flooding his fields. Damaging his sun sheets," Pop said. "Three more years of similar incidents followed until he decided he had enough. No one sees him much now. Likes to keep to himself."

"This mayor of yours, he not like him?" Reyen asked.

Pop shrugged.

"Because it just seems to me that his bad luck might have started with a detonation or two," Reyen said.

Ma went to the cupboard, grabbing up the silverware and plates roughly, and started placing them on the table. "Lyn, go check on the animals," she said with the same roughness.

"I already did," I said, but Pop gave me a look that had me putting on my coat again and leaving the house. I didn't leave the porch, though. Instead, I cupped my ear to the keyhole, tried to ignore the noise of the rain, and listened in.

"If you don't say something, Gael, I will," Ma said.

"Reyen's moving on soon, Tarry. Our affairs are not his."

"He asked, didn't he?" I could hear her moving around. Picking stuff up. Putting stuff down. "McClusky ran for mayor three years ago," she finally said. "He came close to winning. My vote went to him. He would have been good for this town. You must understand, every crop is a Godsend here, and McClusky always had a good crop prior. So, him losing his crop year after year worried everyone." She paused here. "It's important to always have enough stored. Preserved. In case we're forced to move on at some point like the other towns. It's why I am more than a little angry right now to think our mayor would have done such a thing."

When I re-entered the house, pretending I was to the barn and back, Ma went quiet. She sat us all down and started dropping food onto our plates like she was trying to make sure it stuck.

***

On Restday, I was happy to find Reyen in the barn, because I had about a hundred stored-up questions for him. He stood near his horse, running his hands over its sleek black coat. Turning as I approached, he acknowledged me with a smile. "Lyn, you almost have him in the shape he was in when I rode him out of Tabletop. I owe you."

"I don't mind taking care of him. And Jenny enjoys having him here."

He stepped from the stall, removed his hat, and placed it on my head. "I'm told you're old enough to ride in the harvest race this year."

I frowned because I didn't want the reminder. "Pop says I got to sit it out one more year. Jenny's too old and we can't afford another horse just yet."

Reyen pulled out an entry form from his coat pocket. "I picked this up yesterday from the post office. It says the rider has to be a citizen. Born and raised here. Doesn't say nothing about the horse though. Entry fee is on me if you agree." He handed me the form.

"You want me to ride your gaming horse, Reyen?"

"Only if you want to, Lyn."

I nodded several times, feeling the excitement rise in me. "But the race is a month away? Does this mean you're staying on here?"

"Just until after the race."

I may have been happier hearing he was staying for a longer stretch than I was about entering my first race. "I'll fill it out and get it back to the post office. What's his name?" I asked, staring down at the entry form.

Reyen paused. "I never thought to give him one. I'll let you name him if you like."

I thought for a bit. "Well, since you want him to get you home, how about Get-me-there."

He nodded. "Perfect, because if I said that once to him, I said it a hundred times. Grab me the saddle and we'll see how you look up there."

I went running for it.

***

The next Restday, while it was still dark, Reyen roused me up early, and we led Get-me-there down the back road and through my dad's fields. His crops were covered tightly in sunsheets as the rain fell steady. It was just coming dawn when we reached the edge and left the rain and mud for the hard-packed sun-dried waste. I sat behind him, in the shade of his leather coat, shielding my eyes from the rising sun. I'd only ever been out in it a few times and it took getting adjusted too. It was warm but not yet hot. Still, the drier air pulled gently at my skin, lifting the wet from me. It was akin to standing near the stove, but a hundred times finer. I heard the rain behind us, but it was so much quieter now. "What will we do if something comes at us?" I asked, readjusting the level of my voice now that there was no need to compete with the rain.

"I'll take care of that," he said as he gripped my arm as I dismounted, to slow my descent, until I landed softly on the dry ground. While he dismounted, I stepped slightly away from the horse and glanced about at the endless brown horizon. Reyen had already gone over the commands with me, but we went through them again just in case I might have forgotten something. I didn't. I knew them all. When satisfied, he hoisted me up into the saddle. "Run him about a mile. Close enough to town so you can veer him back into the rain if necessary."

I nodded, taking up the reins, which were simply an old west touch. The horse was entirely voice activated.

When Reyen removed his jacket, I spotted the silver handle of a weapon. It made me feel better. Not for myself so much. I at least had speed under me, but Reyen looked somewhat vulnerable standing there.

"Get going. The day will only get warmer. Run him at a fair speed. Don't go any higher. Your Ma will kill me if you fall from him." Reyen adjusted the brow of his hat down over his eyes.

I gave the horse its first instruction. It turned and broke into a gentle, leisurely canter. Even after I crossed the half-mile mark and turned back, the horse was still completely at ease in its stride. His breathing as regular as if he still stood in his stall. I hoped I sat properly. I hoped I looked like a fine enough rider. I wanted Reyen to tell me to run him faster.

Reyen pulled out his weapon then and pointed its long silver barrel at me. All thoughts of Race Day vanished. When he fired, it made no sound at all, but a flare streaked upward and over my head. A screech sounded behind me and I looked back as a large dart bird landed with a loud thud. Its waxy yellow wings still twitching.

Reyen re-holstered his weapon as I brought Get-me-there to a stop in front of him.

"How was that? You want to try a tad more speed?" he asked, smiling.

I looked back at the bird again. Its talons were the size of my head. Every warning I ever received about the Drylands, was all true. I turned back to Reyen and nodded. "Yes, more speed, please."

***

On Harvest Day, several large white tents strung with sunlights were set up in the town's square. Under these tents, there were games of chance and games of skill, and the judging of everything worthy of judging, from pie-baking to quilt-making to squash size to singing voices. There were food stalls and cook-offs already filling the air with mouth-watering smells. The Harvest Day dance would end the day, along with the distribution of prizes and a long-winded speech from Mayor Atkens.

The day began, however, with the race, and the parade route was already crowded with spectators. They stood beneath the tent awnings, in the rain, or on their porches as the procession of horse and rider made their way down Main Street to the starting line.

Martin Chi on Charger led this procession, and a great cheer rang out for the town's unbeaten champions. Following Charger were twenty-three other horses and riders. Some mounts remained calm. Others pranced and sidestepped through the mud. While still others appeared on the verge of bolting, each time the cheers hit a particular pitch. Suzanne Ferguson's horse, Son, was one of them. He had placed second the previous year and doing so he had landed Suzanne a significant chunk of the combo bet. Few betted on Son because most thought such a high-strung horse would burn itself out by the first turn. He hadn't. He came in second by a nose. The combo bet was the only bet that mattered. A bet placed on any two horses in the field, either to win or to place. It didn't matter in which order, although Charger always came in first. Always won the big purse, but for the combo bet to pay up it was about picking the second horse correctly. Once the town folk heard I was riding Reyen's horse, many came around to the house and barn, hoping for a look. Pop was great at making up excuses about why that wasn't possible.

By this point, the vast majority of the town had begun to respect Reyen as a quiet, hardworking, stoic figure, who was quick to nod, share a few words or help in some small way. The long hours and hard labour appeared to have little effect on the tall northerner. He took it in stride, appearing appreciative of having a place to rest up before moving on. If working in the shoulder-high irrigation ditches from sunup to sunset was rest, then it was hard to fathom what he must have already endured.

Jay, who worked in the ditches too as a punishment for some physical altercation he had with one of the town council members, lauded Reyen for saving his life when a valve mistakenly opened, flooding the ditch they were working in.

For these reasons, many in the town were growing uncomfortable with how Reyen was treated by the mayor, and so were hoping secretly that his horse would fare well in this race, although many didn't want to waste a bet on him because Ace Potter had witnessed Reyen riding into town that first night and was adamant that it would take far more than six weeks for an animal in such shape to gain back any true stamina or speed. Not to mention it most likely hadn't encountered much mud in its life.

Still, it appeared the entire town was now stepping out onto the roadway to get a glimpse at this newest addition to the race. We were at the end of the procession, in the twenty-fourth spot, and were only now approaching the crowd. I sat straighter in the saddle. Get-me-there was as cool as a cucumber beneath me. I could now hear the cheers that were directed at me.

"Young Lyn's going to show them how it's done."

"Now that's a lot of horse for a girl's first race."

"Godspeed, Lyn."

"Make your momma proud."

Truth was I was terrified. Not of running. Jenny was a more difficult ride, and she was ancient. Get-me-there was smooth, always went where I told him to go and always gave more when I asked. He never shied or veered. No, I was fine riding Get-me-there. What terrified me was losing. Three days ago, I wasn't. I knew we would most likely come in at least a sound second. I figured we would even give Charger a proper challenge. I was even hoping we might win if everything went perfectly. But then Pop sat me down last night and confided in me what was at stake.

***

As Pop told it, Reyen started to circulate a bit of a brag around town about how tough his horse was for getting him through the Drylands. He even bragged that Get-me-there would win the Harvest Day race. Some tried to convince him that was impossible, but when he remained adamant, they made some small, friendly bets with him that he would lose to Charger. When the mayor got wind of this, he wanted in on the action, and bet Reyen two weeks of provisions if Get-me-there won, and if Charger won, Reyen would work two additional weeks for the mayor in the ditches.

Reyen agreed.

The mayor perhaps thought Reyen had agreed too readily and asked if he wanted to up those stakes?

"Sure," Reyen said. "I'll throw in my horse, if you do the same."

This produced a deep laugh from the mayor. "My horse is a much finer steed than yours, I'm afraid."

That was when Reyen pulled from his rucksack two rare gems, which he had taken from Tabletop. A multi-coloured ammonite, and a lavender-coloured sapphire. "I won't part with my horse if you aren't willing to part with yours," he said. "But I will bet one of these for extra provisions."

Mayor Atkins's sight remained on the gems for a long time before he finally nodded. "How about both?"

"Can't."

"Tell ya what I'll do. If you throw both those stones, plus your horse in the pot, I will place my horse in it too."

Reyen hesitated. Garrett pushed. "Shouldn't go about bragging if you're afraid of a real wager."

"Okay, I'm in." Reyen shook the mayor's hand.

Once Ma heard this story, she made sure as many people as possible knew too, in order to force the mayor to acknowledge that his horse was indeed part of this wager when asked. Many of the citizens wanted nothing more than to see Reyen leave with Mayor Aktens's most prized possession, but few put any money down on it.

***

And this was why I was terrified. If I lost, Reyen would lose his horse. His only means of reaching his family.

Charger was a half hand higher and at least a hand wider than Get-me-there. I hoped in the gaming world that size didn't mean the better mount. If it did, at least Martin was a good fifteen stones heavier than me. Hopefully this might swing things back in our favour.

I was the last to get in line. My heart was beating behind my ears as I strained to hear the bell. The horses pranced and splashed. The rain fell soft and steady. There was a delay as Suzanne got Son under control and behind the line again. Through it all, Get-me-there and Charger stood perfectly still, like bookends, waiting on their voice command. When the bell rang, all twenty-four horses leapt forward. I kept Get-me-there a slight distance behind the front runners and watched as Charger quickly ran away from the pack. I did as Reyen instructed. He wanted Martin to remain comfortable, believing there wasn't any challenge coming his way. And it was working because Martin barely glanced back at the rest of the field as he turned the first corner onto River Road.

I asked Get-me-there for more speed in increments. By the time we turned onto Back Road, I had long passed Son and was now bearing down on Charger. I couldn't make out Martin's expression through the rain when he finally noticed us coming, but Charger suddenly pulled away. I could only hope that he was now at full speed.

I gripped the reins, leaned a little more forward, and asked for full speed too. We were soon pulling up alongside Charger. The horses were breathing heavily now, mud spraying in all directions. When we finally left Back Road to turn onto Main Street again, Get-me-there was within a nose of Charger's. The cheering crowd, the rain, the sound of hooves slapping water were now all a buzz in my mud-caked ears. Charger suddenly pulled ahead again, which meant he hadn't been on full speed. I was crestfallen, for I had no higher speed to ask for. I asked anyway. "Full speed," I repeated. There was no surge. No increase. He was indeed at max. The finish line was closing in and we fell a half-length behind. A length. A length and a half. With no further gaming commands left to utter, I bent lower against his neck and yelled, "Get-me-there." And I swore I saw his ears flick up as if he heard and recognized his name. I yelled it again. Louder and thrill-like. Over and over. Hoping to appeal to that small part of this horse that was still a horse. Hoping his heart would hear me. I felt the shift almost immediately. It came in a slight stumble, which he corrected before offering one last burst of speed, stretching out his stride, flattening out his ears, to charge down Charger. We passed over the finish line a nose ahead.

A wave of exhaustion filled me, receded, and then filled me again as Get-me-there slowed to a lope and then to a walk. Reyen was grabbing up the reins that I must have dropped. Get-me-there was now snorting and prancing slightly. Acting now more like a real horse than he had prior. Reyen spoke softly to him, bringing him to a stop. Ma and Pop approached, along with a wave of town folk, all smiling up at me as the rain fell on them. There was still a roar in my ears, and I couldn't make out a word anyone was saying. I just smiled, knowing I looked more mud than girl.

The mayor immediately made a case for disqualification, stating that we did not inform the race commission that it was a gaming horse. That the rightful winners were Charger and Son in that order. His case was immediately denied by the commission, since there was a gaming horse entered for the last ten years without it ever being stated as one. The mayor then tried to argue that non-citizens weren't allowed to benefit from our town in any form, but since he had failed to call this out prior to the race and had even engaged in a wager with this non-citizen, this was thrown out as well. Nothing he argued worked and fearing that he might resort to more nefarious means, the town folk made sure Reyen received his winnings and then took turns keeping vigil outside our house so no harm would come to him.

***

Reyen left the Monday following. We equipped Charger with enough provisions and water that making it to Greendale was a real possibility for him now. Hopefully, the bridge was cross-able. It was difficult to say how things would go once on the other side. Get-me-there stood saddled and was looking over his shoulder at Jenny. He picked up his ears and nickered softly. She nickered back.

I stood there holding the reins, wishing he were my horse. Wishing I was older. Wishing I had the courage to go with them. Part of me even wished Reyen might change his mind and stay on.

But he only placed a hand gently on my shoulder. 'I owe you and your parents my utmost gratitude. You thank them again for me, okay, and give your Ma this. Just in case you ever need to negotiate.' He handed the sapphire to me. I nodded, knowing he meant in case the rain stopped and we needed to move on to other parts.

"And tell your Ma to stop complaining about the state of things and run for mayor. If there's ever a time. This would be that time." He smiled.

"You think you might ever get back this way?" I reluctantly handed him up the reins.

"Hard to say. But if I find a true path north, I'll get word to you folks. Somehow. I promise." He led the two horses out of the barn and into the rain.

I watched him go, holding him to that promise.

Hell's Bells

Cass Sims Knight

Cass lives in Portland, OR with her pets, who are not pulling their weight on social media. Her fiction has appeared in several magazines, including Stupefying Stories and Drunk Monkeys. You can find her on social media @scifisibyl or at cassandrasimsknight.com.

The ground gave way under Belle's weight. Not a deep trap, but the brush-covered hole in the ground was enough to throw Annie from the safety of her saddle. These were the kinds of traps rumored to be set by hill people to rob passersby. Covered with burlap and a generous coating of dust from the trail, the trap's intention was to break her horse's leg.

Annie opened her eyes and saw the underbelly of trees. She could hear voices cascading over each other in a flurry of disconnected narratives. Some way forward, the men attached to the voices were silently lying in wait behind a cluster of boulders. But Annie could still hear their violent plans. This here canyon was Hillside Gang territory, stretching across the Doomsea Badlands from New Frisco to Quarterlane.

Even in her addled state, she knew they weren't speaking out loud;their thoughts spilled over each other like dough being kneaded for bread. They were screaming in her head. Annie had been thrown from Belle before, but never resulting in disembodied voices swimming around her brainpan. She could tell the malfeasants were still a ways off, having set several traps across the valley.

To stem the panic rising in her chest, Annie focused on the

concrete by doing a quick survey of herself and Belle in search of broken bones. The horse had thrown a shoe from the trap, so even if Annie could muster on, Belle needed looking after. The last town she passed was a ride Belle could make without a shoe. Grasping the reins, Annie swiftly goaded her horse down the rocky hill back the way she had come before the hill people came out of their hiding spot looking for her.

***

The plague of voices hit her like a tidal wave as she neared the edge of town, as if the fall was a crack that had opened a floodgate. Annie's mama always called her intuitive because she knew when it was going to rain or when neighbors were going to stop by, but this was something else altogether. Always kind of a loner, the company of men was even harder now. They had always looked at her like a kid looked at sweets in a candy shop. Except now, she could hear the flavor of ice cream as she walked down the street.

After dropping Belle off at the smithy, Annie made her way over to the saloon, where a wave of voices and images hit her like a warm draft from a mine. She took a step back and tried to block them out, with slim to moderate success.

She considered turning around, but she hadn't had a drink in two weeks and had a powerful thirst. In her experience, she had a fifty-fifty chance of getting in and out of any saloon without incident, odds she'd take any day for a bourbon. Pulling the brow of her hat low, she made her way to the bar.

"Bourbon and something to eat if you got it. Anything will do."

The barman looked at her quizzically, like he wasn't quite sure if she was all there or not. The first day she realized women had a tougher time being invisible, Annie started wearing pants and short hair to fade into the background.

"Percy can whip up some leftovers from the whores' dinner," the barman said, motioning with his chin to the second level, where women in various levels of fine undress watched over the men, like life-sized dolls. These rural whorehouses were usually the only place in town to get a drink.

A gruff man in a duster and spurs sat down next to her, his thoughts becoming louder than everyone else's. Annie's brain became pickled by the flash of images: whores and farm girls, a string of dust covered faces with rivers of salt. Despite herself, she gagged, which did not improve the barrage of images, as now her head appeared at the top of the women. She had met this kind of man before. She didn't need the moving pictures in his head to figure out what he was thinking, and she sure as hell didn't appreciate it. She was going to need to practice her poker face if this new conundrum continued.

Retrieving her bourbon, Annie saw the man had turned to her.

"You got a problem, son?" he asked.

Annie gritted her teeth and shook her head.

"What's that? I didn't hear you."

Annie held up her whiskey in salute before drinking down half.

"What's a matter, son? Cat got your tongue?"

"No, sir," she replied, avoiding eye contact. Annie had a deep voice for a female, but there was no mistaking it for a man's. His eyes narrowed and then widened again in recognition of her feminine character hiding behind the masculine dust and hat.

The outfit usually let her fade into the background if she managed to limit verbal interaction.

"Well, I'll be, an unaccompanied girl. Looking for work, sweetheart? Don't you know the whores stay on the second level? You ain't going to get any johns dressing like that."

"I ain't no whore."

"Aw, little lady," he said, condescendingly, "I'd be honored to be your first john." Annie made eye contact for the first and last time. Silently, she moved down two stools. His attention on her intensified the images she was bombarded with. His pride sickened her. "You ought to pay a man a little respect, jezebel."

She grimaced at the deluge of pornographic close-ups from his head. Annie's mama always said her mouth didn't have the sense her brain gave her. So, naturally, she couldn't resist.

"Defiling farm girls and whores don't make you a man."

He looked at her suspiciously and got up to stand uncomfortably close, breathing heavily as he imagined slicing her from cervix to cranium. Not an image she'd be forgetting anytime soon.

"You think about cuttin' on me again and I will end you," Annie said calmly, keeping her gaze on the liquor bottles behind the bar and making sure to brush back her coat to reveal her Colt pistol.

The man lowered his rotting teeth to ear level. "Witch."

He didn't budge for a full minute before he retreated to the poker game in the corner. Annie watched out the corner of her eye as he leaned in and said something to a well-dressed man sat in the corner with what looked like a table of high rollers. In Annie's estimation, he looked to be a little fish, drunk on the power in his little pond. Most likely the proprietor of this here saloon and, typically, the exact kind of man Annie made a point to avoid.

The well-dressed gentleman looked Annie over, saying something to the jerk from the bar that made him smile. In the din of the packed saloon, Annie couldn't quite place what was going on inside their heads among the din of the rest of the room, but the look on their faces told her all she needed to know. Annie stood and left money on the bar for the bourbon and uneaten meal, the poker players' eyes on her as she walked through the door.

***

She didn't make it ten paces.

When Annie woke up, her head ached, and a man with her antique Winchester dozed in the corner of a barn. He smiled a mite as his mind danced a half dream. When she closed her eyes, all she saw was a spit with her on it. The back of her neck turned red with rage. *Hell's bells*, she thought, *what a pig*.

"What did you call me?" he asked, standing.

Annie's focus shot to her captor, who could apparently now hear what she was thinking as well. *What's the next blow to the noggin' goin' get me?*

"Did you say something, you trollop?"

Trying to push his brain away from hers, she tried to see if she could put up some kind of mental dam to control the flow of thought in his direction. He stood waiting for her to answer. *Fat bastard*, she thought, trying to keep it contained to one head. Nothing, not even a flinch. Annie presumed that to be evidence of her restraint.

"I didn't say nothing."

The man sat back down. *Not a very useful gift*, she decided.

"What you planning on doing here, Hoss?" she asked, fingering the knots of her restraints behind her back.

"Shut up, she-devil. You waiting for your stake."

"How original," she replied. He spat in her face while planning his way with her. "You are a chivalrous man and would make anyone a lucky lady."

He slapped her with the backside of his hand. Annie tasted iron and spat it out. The back of her ears flared into a bright red color, but her expression remained stony. She just couldn't help herself. "You hit like a girl," she informed him.

He wrapped his enormous paw around her jaw, squeezing her cheeks viciously. "You keep this up, little lady, and I'll show you what kind of man I am. You may not be much more to look at than my breeding bitch, but you'll do." He shoved back on her face, almost knocking her back in the chair.

Righting herself by applying outward pressure to the ropes around her wrists and regaining balance, Annie scoffed.

"Now, as much as I enjoyed that charming anecdote of bestiality, I already know what kind of man you are," she said. *Or did you think I couldn't see inside your head?* He started to panic.

"You really are a witch," he said, startled at first, before rushing at her with the butt of his gun. She swiftly lifted her foot toward his crotch, so hard it connected with a crunching noise, counting her blessings that they'd underestimated her and hadn't tied up her feet too. When the man landed on his knees, she smiled for a second before placing her feet on the ground and spinning the lightweight chair around to his face. Luckily, it broke both itself and his nose.

"Sometimes dogs do get their day," Annie leaned over and whispered hoarsely. Her captor got up shakily to swing at her again, but his watering eyes were awash and he swung a full foot from her head. While he was off balance, Annie grabbed hold of his head and brought her knee to his bloody muzzle. He went limp. After tying him up, she did a quick search for her saddlebags, which she'd had on her at the saloon. She found them, crumpled in the corner without her spare pistols. She took her watchdog's pistols, her Winchester, and whatever ammunition she could find. Prior to the saloon, she had left Belle with the blacksmith and could only hope that was where she would find her.

Cracking the door open, rifle cocked, she saw a boy of about twelve. He had been stuck in a boy's fantasy, facing the opening of the alley, ready to draw. Annie walked out calmly, her sights on him.

Speaking just over a whisper, she greeted him, "Who are we today, son? Calamity Dean? The Doomsday Kid?" He spun around, hand on his pistol. She recognized him from when she dropped Belle off at the blacksmith's. "I wouldn't if I were you. I don't want to shoot you, but I will."

Annie could feel his fear beating her brain like the river on a barge, but at least he didn't picture her gutted or naked in restraints. "Boys become men when they learn cruelty," she said cryptically.

They stared at each other in silence for a moment before his hand rose up off his pistol into the air.

"I don't quite understand, ma'am," he said politely. "Is that a question?"

"The question lies in what you was learning sitting out here while that dog had me in there."

The boy's brain worked slowly, grindingly, but to his credit, his mind didn't turn to violence once. He stood there like a prairie dog on his haunches.

"You the blacksmith's son? You remember me from earlier?"

"Yes, ma'am."

"Ma'am, I like that. My horse still at your daddy's?"

"I think so."

"Do you know who jumped me?"

"I don't know which fella did the jumping. I just know it was Mr. Grayson who did the telling."

"He the dapper gentleman from the saloon?"

The kid thought for a moment before he ventured, "Maybe? Mr. Grayson wears a lot of fancy suits. He kind of runs things around here."

"He got any sort of reputation?" Annie asked.

The kid immediately thought about the time he peered into Mr. Grayson's office window and saw a human head on display. It was all Annie needed to know about the man.

"Mr. Grayson is a good boss to my daddy," the kid replied sheepishly.

"Alright boy, get in the barn." The boy seemed harmless, but that didn't mean Annie was stupid enough to just let him go. Inside, she secured her young captive on the wall opposite her previous captor, still unconscious.

When Annie saw the boy eyeing her pistols as she tied him up, she said, "Keep quiet or I'll shoot your daddy as soon as they come running for me. You understand?"

"Yes, ma'am," he replied, the scared boy poking through in his tone.

"Such a little gentleman," Annie commented, squeezing his cheek.

Annie secured the barn door behind her and headed down the alley, away from the main drag. She inched her way along buildings and under windows, peeking around every corner and scurrying across alleys. Just as she snuck through the rear entrance of the stable, she heard the front door creak open. Crouching down, Annie slipped into an empty pen across from Belle, closer to the low, dulcet tones of voices for the proper dropping of eaves.

The possibility occurred to Annie that her newfangled powers might work on animals too. She could see Belle from the door in the corral on the right. *Belle, girl, can you hear me?* Annie's horse lifted her head from the afternoon snack and perked her ears in Annie's direction. Not a thought so much as a warm, fuzzy feeling coming from the animal. *Stay there and be quiet.*

Mr. Grayson came in with his arm around the blacksmith's shoulder.

"She's a witch and we must burn her, but it does smart a bit to waste such a fine animal. It is not the poor beast's fault she was bought by a demon from hell. You'll take care of it?"

"Yes, Mr. Grayson."

As he held his hand out to stroke Belle's nose, the horse reared up slightly and came down in a huff. "Such a shame," he said.

Grayson reflected fondly on the string of women he'd set fire to while the blacksmith thought about his son, regretting the boy's recruitment to Grayson's posse. Neither of them thought of Annie, giving her the opportunity to silently sneak up on Grayson and place her pistol to the back of his head.

"Turn around slowly," she instructed, nudging him with her pistol to show she meant business.

"Ah," he said with an arrogant smile, "speak of the devil and she shall appear."

"You don't need to speak to summon the devil. I can see how he works in you. Now shut up and get on your knees." Both men slowly started to kneel. Without moving the gun pointed at Grayson's head, she looked at the blacksmith and said, "Not you. You get my horse out of her pen."

He froze mid-crouch and said, "I haven't had a chance to reshoe her yet."

"Do I look like I'm in a patient mood?" Annie replied with a steely gaze.

He shook his head and quickly shuffled back toward Belle's pen.

"And throw my saddle on her," she said as he shuffled by with his hands still in the air.

"You won't get away with this, you know," Grayson said.

"Get away with what, exactly?" Annie asked. "Taking

what's mine and leaving town? Didn't realize there was a law against that."

"'Thou shalt not suffer a witch to live.' Our town is a pious one and we will not allow the corruption of the witch to fester across the Badlands."

"Jeeesus, which version of the Bible did you get stuck with? You know witches were invented during the Black Plague? Single women and their cats weren't getting sick because the cats killed all the vermin with fleas on them? Whereas the 'superior sex' was dying in droves because they lived in filth? That ain't witchcraft, that's hygiene."

"The Word is sacrosanct," Grayson replied, his neck turning red.

"You know the bible wasn't written in English, right? So, like a game of telephone, you ain't reading the 'Word', but someone else's interpretation."

Anger flashed in his eyes at being challenged. "We will hunt you down."

"You can try," Annie said as the blacksmith came forward and handed her Belle's reins. "But I'm beginning to wonder if witchcraft doesn't just have its perks."

Just as Annie took the reins, the door swung open and the man from the saloon came in, smiling. When he saw Annie holding a pistol to Grayson's head, a scowl replaced that smile.

In one deft motion, Annie swung her pistol around and shot the man in the head as he went for his pistol. She swung herself up onto Belle's back as Grayson got up from his knees, making for the rifle perched in the corner. Annie reached out to her horse and thought, *Buck*. Belle kicked up her back legs just as Grayson passed behind her, landing one hoof square on his head, blood pooling into the saw dust that covered the floor around his head. As Belle cantered over to the doors, Annie kicked the blacksmith as he tried to swing them shut on her.

Hell's Bells, she thought again, riding toward the setting winter sun.

Out to Pasture

Juliet Kahn

Juliet Kahn is a writer, editor, and bookseller living in Somerville, MA.

Concepcion stares at the turtle in Counselor Jenna's grab-and-go tank. Some idiot paid thousands of dollars to become an animal best known for carrying salmonella and dying in classroom terrariums over summer vacation. She's very nearly awed. She wonders what she's sick with; the grab-and-go tank only comes out for serious cases. She imagines dying, for a second time, as a turtle. She hopes Counselor Jenna will have to deliver the news herself to the doubly bereaved family. Counselor Jenna does not like it when she stares at the other guests like this, but Counselor Jenna has brought the cheap shampoo again, so she can go to hell. Concepcion's spite is thin, though, because she cannot stop herself from doing her awful little dance, that step-step-step that means something might be going wrong inside her legs. She lives in fear of laminitis, which could reduce the gigantic, beautiful, stupid chandelier of her body to mush. She lives in fear of Counselor Jenna's laminitis checks. She hates to have her hooves touched. She hates to smell Counselor Jenna's freesia body splash.

"Calm down, Mrs. Garcia," Counselor Jenna says, smoothing her narrow little hands down her forelimbs. "Just let me get a look at those hooves. And please, don't stare at Mrs. Keene like that. Can you keep your eyes forward for me, Mrs. Garcia? Can you keep your eyes on Mrs. Smythe-Patrick's tail?"

Mrs. Gretchen Smythe-Patrick is an Arabian, like all the Anglo women at Artemisia Ranch who died with terminal degrees and multiple pairs of palazzo pants. Breast cancer, of course. Concepcion feels an obscure pride in her death by uterine cancer; it has a certain mystique, that baroque inflorescence of destruction. It has a certain elegance. She was fifty-five, felled by genetic caprice. She hadn't eaten so much as a single croqueta in years, in service to her culo and then to her scintillating arteries. No smoking, one drink every Nochebuena, four miles on the treadmill five mornings out of seven. Uterine cancer had to fight hard for every inch it conquered. It had to be ingenious.

"Calm *down*, Mrs. Garcia," Counselor Jenna says. She's not wearing gloves. She probably hasn't even washed her hands. She probably woke up ten minutes before she was due to leave and doused herself in overzealous florals. Concepcion resolves to spend the following day whinnying under the director's office window in protest. Gretchen flicks her tail, then takes a shit, right there in the stable.

***

Luis, who was an idiot, insisted upon a bird. "Who doesn't wish they could fly?" he mewled, rifling through Artemisia Ranch's lustrous information packet. He pointed to a photo of a swan, gliding across the ranch's central lake. "Concepcion. Look how beautiful."

"I don't care about flying." Concepcion shot a terse little glance at the ranch's liaison. Could you ask the nurse about that electric blanket? I have chills."

Jerry—or Gary—smiled, which bunched the taut upholstery of his face into something nearly obscene. Once he was gone,

Concepcion turned to her husband. "Say what you mean," she hissed in Spanish. "The stables cost more than the lake."

Luis smiled in the melting way he'd recently developed, which meant *my wife is dying of uterine cancer and I am here for her*, and also, *I will speak in English so people in the chemo suite can hear me being here for her.* "Coño, Concha. It's not about that."

Jerry-or-Gary returned with the electric blanket, which he tucked around Concepcion's shoulders. "Still set on spending your afterlife as a horse, Mrs. Garcia?"

"Yes." Concepcion tucked her chin into the flannel, which smelled of egg bagels, and closed her eyes. "If he says otherwise once I'm dead, it's on you. You're the witness, now."

A half-chuckle limped from Luis's mouth. "A joke."

"It's not." A breath passed through her. "A horse, or nothing." Then, for good measure: "Un caballo o nada."

***

Concepcion's daughter is so pretty. She is beautiful, too, but what Concepcion cannot bear being unable to communicate is her prettiness. Beauty is deep, strange, and a little bit rotten, but prettiness is useful. It delights, rather than stirs. This is so very goddamn rare, and yet, Rosa is wearing an anklet, like a tramp. Concepcion taps out "ARE YOU USING THE NIGHT CREAM WITH THE LEMON." Rosa pretends to be absorbed in her ruthlessly groomed daughter.

Concepcion loves her grandchildren, but only at a distance. She wishes Rosa would not bring them. They are insipid and lazy, which isn't their fault; Concepcion's father was in their mold. "Your father sees a leaf and sees a leaf," her mother always told her. "He sees a pretty woman and sees a pretty woman. He looks, you see him look, you know about it, but that's the end of it. It's wonderful."

Indeed, Concepcion would have preferred a Luis bereft of subterranean desires and his thousand ways of affirming that he is the repository of true feeling in every room. But in a child, it is embarrassing, and in a girl, it is a liability. Madison (*Madison*, carajo) once produced scalding tantrums, which, in retrospect, were promising. But puberty melted them away into emotional and intellectual supinity. Now she mumbles her way through a description of a recent math test (pre-algebra, B-) and a slumber party. "THAT'S NICE," Concepcion taps out. "ROSA ARE YOU USING THE NIGHT CREAM."

"Don't, Mami." Rosa frowns. "You know you're not supposed to."

"THEN WHY DO YOU COME."

Rosa's heartbreaking face furrows. She glances down at Madison, to confirm she's thrown over her reborn abuela in favor of the same three apps she spends eighty percent of her waking life within, then glances back up. "So you can know your grandchildren," she hisses in Spanish. "Should I even bother bringing Manny in next week?"

Concepcion does not say no, though she cannot stand who Manny is becoming. He is handsome. This is convincing him that the fulfillment of his desires is the principal axiom of a just universe. He looks at his stupid sister as if she is his stupid sister, as if he is not every atom as spiritless. Beautiful Rosa. Beautiful Rosa, decanting the wine of herself into collectible McDonald's juice glasses.

Concepcion lets her daughter rub her side like she wants to, and even press her cheek against it. "I'M NOT BLACK BEAUTY," she doesn't tap out. "I AM YOUR MOTHER." She feels her daughter's breath warm her flank, feels her little hand on her withers.

**

Concepcion shifts herself from one hoof to the next as Counselor Eric brushes her, just to make it hard. She sends contradictory messages through the hoofbeat alphabet. It's only supposed to be used in emergencies; to employ it regularly would defeat the purpose of transferral. *You have decided to seize a wonderful opportunity,* the brochures say, *one that humanity has only been able to dream of, until now. In transferring your consciousness to a non-human animal, you will experience non-human cognition. How fully you embrace that will determine the quality of your afterlife.* Concepcion stomps out "YES," "HELP," "I FEEL BAD," "HUNGRY," "NO MORE FOOD," "SHUT UP." The boy sighs.

He also does a bad job with Gretchen, who does not so much as whicker. Trims the mane too high, gets rough with the curry comb. The kind of mistakes a kid already framing this job as a charmingly eccentric chapter of his youth is prone to making. He looks uncomfortable in her lovely, whitewashed stall, at least. It's free of human accouterments, which always surprises Concepcion. They don't advertise it, but paying a little extra will get you a favorite rug or a photo of your kids. Before Parkinson's claimed her, Bethany Chang slipped some groundskeepers a few fat checks to keep her updated on her tennis-playing son's marriage. Concepcion sees them sometimes: a long-lashed deer, fervidly scanning tabloids proffered by women in coveralls.

Counselor Eric finishes Gretchen off with a too-rough pat on the croup, then checks his chirping phone. He arranges his class schedule to make Thursday night the beginning of the weekend. The director doesn't think to tell security to keep an eye out on Thursdays, so Artemisia Ranch fills with more and more kids as the semester wears on. They lie out in the meadow, making up excuses to touch each other. Occasionally, they swim in the lake. The swans box the director's ankles on Friday morning, but nothing ever changes.

Counselor Jenna nudges open the door. She's all feigned insouciance and rolled-up RANCH STAFF t-shirt sleeves, but mostly she is a scraped knee waiting for the balm of Eric's gaze. Her eyes follow him from the comb rack to the shampoo bin.

"Anyone cool coming by tonight?" she asks.

Eric shrugs. "Everyone who usually comes by."

And so she will fill the night air with her limp little jokes and terrible pranks, which are all just different ways to light things on fire. Concepcion stamps out "HUNGRY, HUNGRY, HUNGRY," but neither one of them seems to notice.

***

"A dog, Mami." Rosa cut her eyes to her father, to stave off any comments about bitches. "You loved Gordita so much. A Havanese!"

"No. A horse."

Rosa sighed. But she was glad, Concepcion knew. She had deep and luminous feelings about women and horses.

Her own mother was less understanding. "Conchita," she creaked. "Mi niña. Just die. This is bullshit."

"Are you saying," Concepcion said, once she'd found her voice in the rubbish pile at the bottom of her throat, "that you truly, actually cannot understand me wanting to live longer. Wanting to see Madison and Manny grow up a little more."

"It would be pathetic." Her mother closed her eyes. "That is what I mean. Rosa and the children, petting you. Watching some boy muck out your shit."

"So you'd rather see me die."

"Yes." Her mother threw up her ancient hands. "Yes, I would rather see you die. That isn't some shocking thing, to me. I'm not in pain saying I'd rather see you die. Yes. I would rather see my daughter die."

***

Gretchen runs every sunny day, and this Friday is no exception. Trash from last night's flaccid bacchanalia has been blown into the ranch's margins, but she doesn't seem to notice, trotting past a Fritos bag like it's an especially vivid autumn leaf. Her husband watches from the side of the meadow. He brings his lunch in special interlocking containers: a small, round cheese, crackers, the bright rubble of chopped fruit. Concepcion can see him, adrift in a house full of his wife. Her kantha quilts. Her chunky wooden jewelry. Her linocut prints, bought at an art fair in which their blue-haired granddaughter exhibited her work. Gretchen's long hands picking up a print of a dandelion, or perhaps a political slogan made anodyne through abstraction: "Nothing about us without us," "Justice for all." Gretchen helping pack up the kid's stuff at the end of the day and taking her to a tasteful restaurant she wishes she was less comfortable within. Gretchen saying, *There's just so much art in the world,* in her birdish voice. *People really are creative, you know? No matter where we go, we just can't help but make beauty. Isn't that great?*

***

The girl was an equestrian. Concepcion sat in her car, watching her take her pretty horse for a ride around campus one Sunday afternoon. The girl went to Rosa's school; Concepcion already had the right sticker on her windshield. Campus police officers walked by her Audi without blinking.

She wanted to ask if she was Rosa's friend. If Luis stayed past the hour when a father might visit his daughter, and if this was how they met. If he looked like an old man to her. But in the end, all she asked was if she was pregnant. If she cried, she waited until Concepcion left.

"A blessing," Concepcion's mother said, her fingers on her daughter's wrist. No one knowing about the dark thing growing inside her, yet.

***

Concepcion wakes to the smell of burning things you're not supposed to burn. Eric and his little friends never manage to find anything but green wood and take-out clamshells to use as bonfire kindling. The kids clatter into shadowy form before her, snickering and shifty.

"Hi horsie," says an acne-curdled boy wearing a faded LET IT BE t-shirt. Eric is behind him, alongside a blonde girl Concepcion doesn't recognize. Then she steps into the light, and she realizes it's Jenna. She looks brittle and hectic, like she's drunk but trying not to be. She busies herself with peering at everything except Concepcion. The boy in the LET IT BE t-shirt makes awful little clicking and spitting noises, like he's trying to get a recalcitrant cat into a carrier.

"Christ," Eric says. "Let me." He reaches into the shadows and rummages crunchily for something.

"Oh, fuck." Jenna puts her face in her hands. "Eric, don't. It's weird."

"Why?" He emerges, and his hands are full of sugarcubes. "She's a fucking horse."

She is. And the sugarcubes' smell is filling every groove of her brain. But Concepcion realizes, as Eric shoots a furtive look out the door, that she doesn't actually hate the idea of following him outside. The kids can thrill to the sight of her, their misfit bonafides made manifest. Who cares. She would like to see the moon over the meadow.

She surprises them by stepping out of the stall. They begin to walk towards the door, flicking little glances at her over their shoulders. Eric's face breaks into a smile. "Fuck yeah!" he hollers as they head for the meadow. The bonfire at its center is so lovely, Concepcion has to stop. It's been so long since she's seen fire. Is this a horse thing? Is she in thrall to the lesser mysteries, with her lesser brain? No: fire is beautiful. It is possible to forget this, even when one has not had their flickering soul-stuff kneaded into the body of a fucking horse.

But oh, to be a fucking horse when the moon is a fat pearl in the sky and the air is cool and the queenly pleasure of obeying one's whims fills every vein. It's like being on the roof of her boarding school after lights-out, watching neon lights prickle the sky's dark belly. It's like leading Rosa past the breakers. That feeling of pushed-out edges, of leashlessness. She breaks into a trot around the pasture's edge, to the kids' whoops. They're shadows, at this distance; clumsy letters in an alphabet she can't read. Perhaps she will forget how to read, at some point. Perhaps she will stop giving a damn, like Gretchen, and shit in front of strangers.

And Gretchen is there. Concepcion doesn't believe it, at first, but as she rounds the furthest corner of the meadow she sees her wintry coat catch the light. Concepcion moves closer, feels her hooves sink into dirt already churned by the pale mare's movements.

"Hey," someone says, all the mirth in their voice beveled with panic. "Hey! Whoa! Shit!"

It's a boy. There's a boy riding Gretchen, his long legs dangling. She goes faster than she probably should, and then a little faster still. The boy keeps laughing, panicking, laughing, his heels nipping at her sides.

***

Concepcion sat at her vanity, dying. It had gained vigor, and deserved distinction. She wanted to vomit all the time and her skin was thin as tissue. That Luis could think she wanted to spend her afterlife as a swan was even more riotous, in light of these developments. An animate meringue, reduced to long-necked slapstick at the slightest disturbance. A horse was dignified even at its most displeased. Its honor couldn't be destroyed, it could only become bladed. It was never less than itself.

She ran a finger down the serrated edge of a tennis bracelet as she examined Artemisia Ranch's catalog. She wanted to be a Friesian, though that felt like a betrayal. A Cuban Criollo breed would be the most appropriate. She could see herself enjoying a second life as a Cubano de Paso, wearing that great raw topaz of a face But Friesians. She couldn't resist their elegiac grace, their eyes like halved moons, their strength. And she wanted her hair back. She pictured herself stranding tall in the ranch's meadows, Queen Anne's lace frothing at her fetlocks. To the trees? To the stables? To the Japanese garden, featuring designated Comfort Copses™ for equine, avian, and reptilian guests? A whole life marshaled in her hooves, waiting for manifestation through the thousand genius movements of her body. A single sunny day, waiting to be devoured.

***

Family and Friends Weekend is always a bit of a disaster. Younger counselors swipe the petit fours labeled EQUINE rather than GUESTS and end up choking on apple butter and julienned hay. Sons mistake someone's pet for their freshly canined mothers. People cry, but never when you expect them to. Concepcion supposes she's gotten off easy with Luis, Rosa, Madison, and Manny assembled on a gingham blanket before her. Rosa is pre-occupied with clenching peace into place, the children are not interesting enough to cause a scene, and crowds have a way of pressing Luis into shape.

Gretchen is with her husband and a small crowd of progeny. Everyone over 40 has the lean, upright look of long-distance cyclists with high-powered jobs. Everyone under 40 is a collection of peachy roundnesses and pulled-taut planes. They're laughing in their little semicircle, passing a bowl of watermelon salad around.

Manny snickers at something on his phone. Madison frowns at her own, and idly picks at a scab. Rosa has taken the bocaditos out of their tinfoil too early. Luis takes one, though. It might be out of fatherly feeling, but he might simply see them. Eating is an entirely animal affair for him: there is no space between desire and action, and no consequences he cares about.

Concepcion paces around them in a slow circle. Luis reaches out to bat at her fetlocks. "Like bell bottoms," he says, around a mouthful of ham and cheese. "Right, Concha? Remember those yellow ones you had, on our honeymoon?"

"Oh, God." Rosa grins. "Papi, tell the story about the pool."

Luis smiles and sits up straighter. "Your mother," he says, "was a very beautiful woman. Oye, Manny. Madison. Escúchame, coño. Your grandmother was a very beautiful woman, when we went on our honeymoon."

And she had been 26, and could do the splits, and when Luis asked her, *Does it sound crazy?* about the ideas she would pinch and roll and smooth into shape, she said, *no*. And he said, *Please don't lie to me. All I ever want is the truth from you.* When his string of snapped-off relationships had been proof of his need of her, rather than a warning she can't believe she didn't heed. But Rosa is glowing and Concepcion just keeps up her slow, careful walk in this body that cannot sit.

"She wore a white bathing suit to the hotel pool," Luis says. "And it was not, ah, expensive. It was not well-made. So when she got out of the water–"

"It was see-through!" Madison's voice, somehow. She laughs. "Right?"

"Yes!" Luis nods. "Yes, and it was a wonderful moment for me, of course–"

"Papi–"

"But I was eager to be a good husband, and so I dove at her with

194

our towel. But she was not prepared." Luis throws his hands up, imitating their titanic splash. "And at that moment, who should be walking behind your beautiful abuela but a helpless hotel employee."

A weedy boy, whose underwater eyes snapped to her nipples. Concepcion whickered, which Luis noticed. He nodded, eyes twinkling. "Yes, yes. All three of us went into the pool."

"And then Mami wouldn't come out," Rosa says. "And you were trying to explain to the employees that you needed a robe for her—"

"But my English was shit, then." Luis inclines his head towards Madison and Manny, both of whom have forgotten their phones. "So what I told them was, 'Please, my woman's breasts are open!'"

Gretchen is trotting. Gretchen is inscribing a line upon the ground. Her husband looks at her, but Concepcion cannot see his expression. She can only see Gretchen trotting, trotting.

"Open!" Luis laughs, Manny laughs, Madison laughs. Rosa looks up at Concepcion, limpid with love and gratitude. To be here, to have stolen her mother back from the abyss, to live in this age of wonders. To be here with this man who got her birthday wrong on the pediatrician's intake form. This man who held her mother's hand as she slipped into that dark alleyway, that thing they said would be an "intermission." That foiled escape. That transformation.

She can smell Counselor Jenna on the air, suddenly. Her winey sweat, the gouda she's ferrying from family to family. And there she is, resting for a moment against the stables. Eric hovers above her, cumulonimbic.

"Concha?" Luis' silly, louche voice. But it cannot scale her legs, suddenly. It cannot climb them, cannot cross the great tilted slab of her body, cannot reach the clever points of her ears.

She begins to trot, then to canter. She heads for Jenna, then finds herself passing her. She enters the meadow.

"Mami!"

The meadow. The pasture. The pond. It's a lovely day, honestly. The swans take clumsily to the air as she passes them. She wants a drink of water until the pond glimmers into view, and then she realizes she isn't thirsty. So she runs on.

"Mrs. Garcia!"

The wind smells like a cut green thing. She starts to gallop. She reaches the edge of the grass, the edge of the staff buildings.

"Mrs. Garcia!"

The parking lot. The gate. There are no more voices, but there is a white smear at the edge of her vision. There is a doubling of her hoofbeats.

Concepcion stops once she reaches Route 2's asphalt and turns. Gretchen is by her side.

Fuck you, Gretchen she thinks, immediately. She turns the phrase over and over again in her mind. It trembles in her hooves, and others join it. *I think these legs will kill me.* And: *I can't bear my daughter's hands.* And: *He wouldn't even let me die alone.*

But she doesn't tap any of them out. She just looks at Gretchen, standing there beside her in the middle of the road.

Rodney's Request

Mary Jo Rabe

Mary Jo Rabe grew up on a farm in eastern Iowa, got degrees from Michigan State University and University of Wisconsin-Milwaukee. She worked in the library of the chancery office of the Archdiocese of Freiburg, Germany for 41 years, and retired to Titisee-Neustadt, Germany. Information about her published stories can be found on her blog: https://maryjorabe. wordpress.com/

Rodney McTavish trotted briskly along the shoulder of Iowa Highway 64 as he headed north. He was pleased with his extended vacation on this new continent. What with often tasty food, varied climate, and fairly safe traveling circumstances, a unicorn from Scotland could easily spend a few pleasant centuries here.

As it was early morning and still dark and foggy, he didn't see any necessity for making himself or any of his body parts invisible. His usually bright, shiny, white coat was a dusty, orangish-brown from the gravel roads he had previously given preference to, making him fairly difficult to see.

Naturally, it was prudent for those of his kind to keep their existence a secret from other life forms on this planet. Fact of existence: Any minority life form will encounter members of a majority who want to harm it. Prevention was always easier and generally more successful than defense.

Complete invisibility, though, was foolishly strenuous, and before he knew where his next meal was coming from, he didn't want to waste the energy.

At the top of the next hill, Rodney thought he saw a farmstead behind a little roadside park. This was all very promising. People often left food in the garbage containers next to the picnic tables, and up at the farm he would most likely find water to drink. He was sure that he heard cattle, and they usually had some kind of trough or other source of water.

He couldn't see well through the fog, and was therefore disappointed when he got to the park. It was much too tidy, with squeaky-clean, sky-blue wooden benches and tables. There weren't any leftovers to munch on anywhere. Even the trash containers were immaculate, not one crumb to be detected. Rodney's stomach growled.

The grass was mowed down to a ridiculous height of less than half an inch. Rodney preferred not to fill his lips with dirt unless he was literally starving, not that he liked to eat grass anyway. It was theoretically acceptable for his equine metabolism but boring; he truly didn't enjoy the taste.

Rodney's quiet neigh now turned into a weary sigh. He turned toward the farm buildings and cantered briskly in their general direction. Whatever animals the farm supported seemed to be asleep in the three-story, creaking, wooden building with a steep roof, flaking red paint, and missing slats. Probably what the locals called a barn in Iowa. He didn't see any cattle or hogs, but he heard muffled lowing and grunting.

Unusually close to the barn stood a two-story, white farmhouse with green asphalt shingles in the middle of a modest lawn surrounded by a flimsy, white, wooden, picket fence. There were no lights in the house and Rodney couldn't detect any canine life forms skulking about. So, this seemed like a safe enough watering hole.

Rodney then trotted over to the trough in the muddy barnyard. Not bad. Fresh, clean water in one trough and acceptably edible, commercial cattle feed in the other. He'd tasted better, but at least it had any taste at all.

Rodney ate and drank enough to make him sleepy, though he was more inclined to blame the distance he had covered this past night. He sought out a safe place for a necessary nap where he couldn't be seen from the road and lay down in a pleasant, grassy ditch behind the barn.

He didn't think he had dozed off for very long, but he gradually woke up in bright sunlight when an immature, human female, a little over one meter in height with a long, blonde ponytail, wrapped her arms around his neck, petted his mane, and said, "Horsey, horsey! I love you, horsey."

Only half awake, Rodney murmured, "Yes, lass. Mind the horn; I dinna want ye to get hurt."

"You talk funny," the little creature said in a squeaky voice as she rubbed her face into his mane.

That startled Rodney enough to wake him up completely. Horsefeathers, flashing back to a time when his kind could fly. Rodney, of course, had never flown, but unicorns had excellent shared memories, and so he often felt the breeze of flight. Maybe that's what kept him traveling, that and an intrinsic discontent.

As a matter of principle and practicality, he had always tried to avoid any kind of confrontation with various, annoying knights in shining armor. Granted, on occasion he had had to impale a few annoying specimens, but always with regret. It was so much work, disposing of the bodies afterwards and trying to get the sticky gunk off his horn.

Anyway, this situation here was already a huge problem. Horsefeathers. Rodney was old enough to know how to avoid trouble. Don't reveal yourself to humans; don't let them see your horn; don't let them know you can talk; don't, don't, don't. And above all, stay away from virgins who have this inexplicable power over you. That's the only way to have a little peace and quiet and enjoy your long life. But, of course, he didn't always abide by these sensible rules.

With respect to the here and now, he first absolutely had to adjust his dialect to Midwest American rural and add the required twang for the times when he might choose to talk. Certainly, the most sensible thing to do would be to turn invisible and gallop away before the little girl made any specific requests.

Unfortunately, the little creature's arms around his neck were so tight that he couldn't shake them loose. And though her thoughts were somewhat jumbled, he sensed that she needed him. She didn't have anyone to talk to. So, for various reasons, he was already under the spell of this little girl.

***

Charlotte bolted upright on her bed, horrified that it was already so late. She must have forgotten to set the alarm. Possible. She had been exhausted last night after a long day of baling hay and had collapsed onto the bed without even undressing. She was only thirty, but some mornings she felt more like ninety.

She felt around for her shoes. Her arms, shoulders, and legs ached with every movement.

She hadn't slept well. Nightmares of Mr. Morton from the bank and her husband Joe's two surviving brothers had tormented her. It wasn't fair. She worried enough about the farm during the day; she didn't need the stress to continue all night.

Childish shrieks of "horsey" coming from behind the barn? She didn't have any horses on the farm. Where was Susie? A sudden irrational fear replaced any pain from sore muscles. Slipping into her worn tennis shoes, Charlotte ran down the stairs, out the rusty, screen door at the front of the house, and past the barn to the little patch of woods.

"Susie," she said. "Where are you? What are you doing?"

Susie let go of Rodney's neck, jumped up out of the ditch, and ran over to Charlotte.

"Mommy, Mommy," she yelled. "I found a horsey, I found a horsey. Can I keep him, please, can I keep him?"

Rodney was slightly surprised at how easily the thin, somewhat fragile-looking woman picked up the little girl. Almost as blonde as her daughter, though with short, wild hair that looked like it had just escaped a threshing machine, the woman stared at Rodney. There was no time for him to suddenly turn invisible, even partially, and now that this child□Susie□controlled him, it would really serve no good purpose.

"Any horse has to belong to someone around here," the woman began as she walked over toward Rodney.

"What on earth is that under the horse's forelock?"

Rodney sighed and stood up. "It's a horn," he said softly in what many damsels in the past had assured him was a comforting, bass voice. "And I'm not a horse; I'm a unicorn."

Charlotte stumbled a few steps backward. Then she turned in a complete circle and looked around.

"No," she said. "There is no such thing. Unicorns, dragons, centaurs, they're all just imaginary. And animals don't talk. Somebody is playing a trick on me."

Rodney sighed to himself. The woman's thoughts were fairly intelligent otherwise, but in some ways she was deplorably ignorant.

Rodney shook his head and whinnied. "I am sorry. I should have been more circumspect. I underestimated how tired I was when I decided to take a little nap behind your barn. I never wanted anyone to see me, and it's actually quite important to me that no one knows I'm here."

"But," he continued firmly, pawing at the grass around the ditch. "I am real. So are dragons, by the way, and you don't ever want to get them annoyed with you."

The woman still looked spooked. Rodney tried to make his voice more soothing and melodious. "I suggest we discuss my presence here like reasonable creatures," he said. "Naturally, I'm willing to leave immediately, if that's what you and your little girl ask me to do. Unicorns never stay where they aren't wanted." This wasn't completely true as unicorns tended to defend their lairs, but there was no need to go into detail.

The child jumped down, ran back over to Rodney, and put her arms around his right foreleg. "Don't go," she said to Rodney.

Susie continued, "I want to keep this horsey. Please let me keep him, Mommy. I want this horsey. He's my friend."

Rodney looked up at Charlotte, afraid that she might do something rash.

"Let me explain my presence here," he said. "Unicorns generally live a long, long time. I got tired of horsing around in Scotland and the rest of the British Isles. Beautiful countries, but after a few centuries I had seen every loch and hill. So I jumped a freighter to North America after the big war, and I have been hoofing it around this continent for several decades. Unicorns can talk, but we tend to be a little hesitant about contact with you human beings. There have been a number of unfortunate misunderstandings in the past." Rodney tried to look humble and non-threatening.

Charlotte shook her head and closed her eyes. She was exhausted and just didn't have the strength to deal with something she couldn't believe but had to admit was standing in front of her. With the bank and her two brothers-in-law trying to take the farm away from her, she really had more pressing problems.

She opened her eyes and sighed. "Well, you're here," she said. "You look like what unicorns are supposed to look like. I hear you talking. Susie says she wants to keep you. So you might as well stay."

Rodney whinnied. "It would be my pleasure to do whatever this little girl wants," he said.

"I can assure you that I am a worthy and ethical unicorn. I would suggest that we come to some agreement about my stay here," Rodney continued. He saw no need to explain that he couldn't leave as long as the little girl wanted him to stay. If people here were that ignorant about unicorns, he wasn't obligated to educate them.

However, he did have to impress upon them the necessity of keeping his presence and existence a secret. Unicorns did have some powers, but in many situations, he would be helpless up against a crowd of human beings. Rodney wanted to survive the next centuries he had ahead of him. He had a lot of traveling to do.

"It would be best if no one else learned that you have a talking unicorn on your farm," he began. "Some of your hunter friends would no doubt love to try to make me a trophy on their walls. Some of your timid friends might be afraid of me."

"I can make my horn invisible for short periods of time, and I won't do any talking if anyone else is around. So, all you have to do is explain to anyone who asks that a strange, stray horse just showed up suddenly on your farm and you're taking care of him. Can you promise to do that?"

Charlotte tried to listen attentively, but what with obsessing about Mr. Morton and her two brothers-in-law and what they were planning, she had too many other things to think about. She managed a distracted nod.

Rodney sighed. There were advantages to reading human minds, but it was often a burden. Charlotte, the little girl's mother, was worrying about many situations that Rodney didn't yet understand.

"I do have a healthy horse's appetite," Rodney continued. "However, I want to earn my keep. I'm not suited for any kind of farm labor, no pulling a plow or chasing cattle. I'm not a beast of burden. However, I might be able to help you with a few suggestions now and then. We unicorns have a limited ability to see into the future, no individual fates and not every detail, mind you, but trends."

Charlotte couldn't really believe that any of this was happening. "Of course," she said, as she tried to prevent feelings of hysteria. "Why shouldn't a talking unicorn from Scotland suddenly show up on my farm and be able to predict the future?"

Rodney tried to appear patient and harmless.

Charlotte didn't know what to do. This was all more than she could deal with at the moment. Her conscious gave her constant guilt about Susie, never having enough time for her, what with trying to farm the two hundred acres by herself. Susie wanted this—whatever it was—as a pet, and it didn't seem threatening, so why not?

"Ok, unicorn," she said. "We have a deal. You can stay, and Susie and I won't tell anyone we have a unicorn on the farm. We'll discuss everything else later. Please excuse me. I have work to do."

Susie ran back to Rodney. "I want to stay with my horsey."

Rodney swished his tail back and forth. "Call me Rodney," Rodney said.

Looking over to Charlotte, he continued, "I hope we can turn this situation into an amicable relationship beneficial to us both." This was true enough especially since he couldn't leave.

The little girl let go of his leg and reached up for his muzzle. Rodney bent down his head, carefully pointing his silver-blue horn away from her. "I'm Susie," the little girl said. "My daddy went to heaven last Christmas. I miss talking to him, but now I have a horsey I can talk to."

Charlotte looked away and Rodney neighed quietly. "Yes, you have a horsey," he told Susie.

Looking up at Charlotte, Rodney added, "I can stick around for a few years. Every century or so I allow myself a little diversion of constant contact with human beings."

Charlotte felt calmer. She actually had a good feeling about Rodney, though she couldn't explain why.

"Rodney," she said, looking at the unicorn. "Maybe you can explain to Susie about keeping your secret. But now it's time for breakfast, and then I have crops and animals to tend to."

Rodney coughed discretely.

"Feel free to eat with the cattle," Charlotte said. "I'll fill up the troughs after I've had something to eat."

"I'll be right back," Susie said. "Wait for me, Rodney."

Rodney returned to his ditch. The situation was not completely satisfactory, but it could be worse.

Charlotte put her arm around Susie's shoulders and walked back to the house with her. The house was just as old and just as dilapidated as the barn. At the moment, however, the condition of the house and barn was the least of Charlotte's worries.

When Joe's father died, he left the farm to Joe and his brothers. Joe borrowed money from the local bank, bought up his brothers' shares of the farm, and married Charlotte. Charlotte, who had met Joe at Iowa State in Ames, had planned to become a home ec teacher, but then learned how to farm instead. They had a few good years when it was easy to make the payments to the bank.

They had Susie, a few more good years, and then Joe was diagnosed with acute leukemia and died six months later. Since then Charlotte tried to run the farm by herself, but the times were no longer good for Iowa farmers.

"Would you like some cereal?" she asked Susie, who had already put her bowl and spoon on the table.

"Hand me the box," Susie said. "I want to go back and play with my horsey."

Charlotte knew that her daughter was just as stubborn as she was. She gave her the box of her favorite brightly colored, fruit-flavored cereal, watched her fill half of the bowl and then pour milk over it. By the time Charlotte had returned the milk to the refrigerator, Susie had slurped down her cereal and run out the front door. Charlotte heard the joyful cries of "horsey, horsey", and then the telephone rang.

"We need to talk, Mrs. Rogers," Mr. Morton's whiny voice made Charlotte want to throw the phone on the floor and grind it into dust, but she couldn't stop listening.

"Your farm account is overdrawn again. Even if you sell your cattle as planned, you won't make enough to make your next loan payment, much less buy new feeder calves. The bank can't carry deadbeats forever. You really need to consider selling the farm to your brothers-in-law. That would keep the farm in the family, which is what you said you wanted."

"After they pay me peanuts for the farm, nothing can stop them from selling it to the highest bidder and disappearing with the money," Charlotte said. She was getting so tired of this conversation.

"They have assured me," Mr. Morton began.

"I don't have time for this now," Charlotte said. "We can talk after I sell the cattle." She hung up and walked out onto the back porch where she could see the fields, all planted and thriving. She liked the view; more to the point, Joe had loved it. She remembered how he had painted the porch swing a bright, bubble-gum pink after Susie had chosen that color.

He had been so proud of the whole farm. The framed certificate from the Historical Society, stating that the farm had been in the Rogers family for over a hundred years, hung in the living room. Susie made Charlotte read it to her every night before she went to bed. That's what Joe had done, and Susie needed the ritual. Charlotte had to keep the farm for Susie.

In the distance, she heard Rodney's deep voice explaining to Susie that she must tell everyone that a horse just showed up one day. She must never mention Rodney's horn, and never tell anyone that Rodney could talk, or Rodney would leave.

Although she hated herself for the thought, Charlotte couldn't help wondering how much the tabloids would pay for a film of a genuine unicorn. Maybe she could even claim rights to all products using unicorns as advertising if she owned the one-and-only certified unicorn on the planet. Then she could save the farm for Susie.

Suddenly Rodney trotted over to the porch, followed by Susie running as fast as her short, little legs would let her.

"Mommy," she said, all out of breath. "Rodney is my horsey and my best friend. I promised him that we would take good care of him."

Rodney stared at Charlotte. "Susie," he said. "Would you run over to the hayfield and pick me some good-tasting stalks? That's what I would really like for breakfast."

Susie ran off, and Rodney said to Charlotte, "Why don't you explain your whole situation to me? Your thoughts are muddled, confused, and distorted with emotion. If I know exactly what is going on, I might be able to give you some practical advice so that you don't have to betray me and, by the way, lose Susie's trust forever."

"How did you..." Charlotte turned pale.

"We unicorns do have some telepathic powers," Rodney said, adding to himself "And damned good hearing."

"My take on your situation is that your brothers-in-law indeed do intend to sell the farm to the highest bidder and have promised that Mr. Morton a fair amount of money if he coerces you into going along. Why don't you just sell the farm to the highest bidder yourself?"

"I can't," Charlotte said and started to cry. "Joe, Susie's father, wanted the farm to stay in the family, and I have to make it possible for Susie, if that turns out to be her choice. I've tried to keep the farm running, but I'm failing. I'm beginning to wonder if it is even possible for an Iowa farmer with fewer than two hundred acres stay in business."

Rodney closed his eyes and scanned various telepathic information sources for a few seconds. Then he said, "Yes, it is. Sell your cattle and hogs and don't get any new ones. You don't have the capacity to be a factory meat farm, and you wouldn't like it anyway."

"Plant more corn. Corn is big. You might also consider growing more hay and alfalfa. I like alfalfa; it is quite tasty. And heather, I miss heather. Sell your crops to the highest bidder, which may often be your neighbors who still raise animals. Rent out the space in your barn to your neighbors."

"Most importantly, find out about government subsidies for not planting your fields."

Charlotte looked slightly hopeful. "I don't know about the subsidies. Joe said he would never do that, but the rest sounds doable. I'm sorry I considered throwing you to the media wolves. I was just desperate. Please don't tell Susie. She would never forgive me."

"Of course not," Rodney said. "But you realize that I will only feel obligated to keep your secrets if you keep mine."

***

Over the years, Rodney gave Charlotte good advice. They got into the habit of talking every night after Susie went to bed. Charlotte became somewhat prosperous and paid off her loans. At Rodney's suggestion, she started running for local office and got elected to the soil and conservation board on her first try. A few years later, she became a state representative.

Susie had a fairly subservient and absolutely loyal unicorn for her best friend. Rodney listened patiently to everything Susie felt like saying. He really couldn't complain□he actually led quite a pampered existence here on the farm□though he often stared off into the distance, longing for far-away places.

Charlotte cleared a spot in the barn for Rodney the first day and made a suitable horse stall out of it. With precise directions from Rodney, she managed to get it right. While Rodney as a civilized unicorn naturally took care of his excretory needs outside the barn, he still required sufficient fresh straw every day along with his trough of fresh water.

Getting the correct food organized for Rodney's gourmet palate took a little longer. The commercial cattle feed was something Rodney was only willing to tolerate in exceptional circumstances. He preferred a mixture of hay, alfalfa, and corn, with fresh fruit for dessert and an occasional treat of heather.

Susie insisted on learning how to take care of her horsey. Charlotte picked up a booklet about the care of ponies and horses from the agricultural extension office in the county seat.

Rodney let Charlotte think he stayed because she and Susie treated him so well, choosing not to mention the fact that he couldn't refuse anything Susie asked for. He sensed that medieval lore, no matter how accurate, wouldn't be understood or appreciated.

With help of a footstool, Susie insisted on brushing Rodney every day, which of course was quite pleasant once she acquired a certain expertise. His coat soon had its original, blindingly white color back. After several years and more than one growth spurt, Susie no longer needed any device to help her care for Rodney.

One cool October evening Susie started talking about making him her 4-H horse and pony project for the County Fair the next summer. Rodney hadn't paid enough attention when she first started babbling about how she had joined 4-H because this cute boy had invited her.

"Susie," Rodney began, trying to hide his alarm. "You know it's hard for me keep my horn invisible for hours at a time. I absolutely can't be an exhibit at any fair." The fact that he couldn't deny Susie anything gave him a definite sense of panic.

"You don't have to," Susie said. "At the fair I just show my records and pictures. You only have to hide your horn for a few minutes when the country extension agent comes to observe me with you."

"Don't worry," Susie said. "The project will just help me learn how to take better care of you."

"Hmm," Rodney answered skeptically.

The taking better care of him part of the project turned out to be true. Susie checked out a stack of books from the school library and read them all to Rodney. She interviewed the local veterinarian twice. She learned how to examine Rodney's teeth, gums, and hooves quite competently. She not only continued to brush his coat every day, she also combed his tail very carefully, removing any snarls or insects or vegetation painlessly.

The problems began in the spring when Susie said she needed to learn how to put on a bridle and saddle, had to be able to mount and dismount, and ride him with a good sense of balance.

"No," Rodney said firmly. "We unicorns aren't beasts of burden; we are free creatures. No one puts a bridle or saddle on a unicorn."

Susie looked sad. "But then I'll only get a white ribbon for my project, and I really want a blue one."

Rodney snorted. "Ribbons."

Susie looked very sad. "Please," she said.

Of course, he couldn't refuse her, though he ground a few layers off his newly polished teeth at the thought of bridles and saddles. This situation was getting less and less bearable.

Being ridden was a most unpleasant activity. Rodney had no idea how horses put up with the indignity of having humans weighing them down, kicking their sides, pulling at their mouths. He was glad that none of the other unicorns could see his embarrassing prancing around the barnyard with an impatient girl on his back.

Fortunately, her riding skills improved with time. After a few months, he hardly noticed her on his back at all. By the time the country extension agent came to evaluate Susie's project in July, she was quite good at putting on his bridle and saddle and riding him around the buildings in the different gaits. However, it was exhausting work for him to keep his horn invisible while concentrating on the steps, and he almost collapsed when the agent finally left.

Fortunately, the man promised Susie a blue ribbon at the fair for her efforts.

"Are you okay?" Charlotte asked Rodney after the extension agent left. "It is so kind of you to put up with Susie's whims. After losing her father, all she had left were two larcenous uncles who never did a thing for her. You have helped Susie so much all these years."

All Rodney could summon up the strength to do was nod.

Using some of the magic at his disposal□unicorns didn't have unlimited supplies of the stuff□Rodney managed to manipulate Susie into believing she wanted to do nutrition and gardening as her 4-H project for the next summer.

Once he no longer had to put up with a bridle and saddle, time went by quickly. One day he noticed that Charlotte's hair had some gray streaks, and Susie spent less and less time at home and more and more time with the cute boy from 4-H. Rodney began to feel more and more restless, though of course still obligated to stay.

One night in November, Charlotte came into the barn after Susie had left with her boyfriend for the junior-senior homecoming dance. Ordinarily Rodney and Charlotte had their business conversations at the house, Charlotte on the porch swing and Rodney rolling around on the freshly mown lawn.

"Rodney," Charlotte began. "Maybe you should try sleeping outside for a while."

"What!" Rodney brayed. "No! This unicorn needs his warm stall with fresh straw. You know that. What's going on?"

"Well, even the sheriff doesn't really have a clue, but someone has been setting barns on fire around here. The maniac comes in the middle of the night, dumps canisters of gasoline in the haylofts and then throws in lit firecrackers from a safe distance, probably from his car. Of course there aren't any tire marks on these gravel roads, and so they don't know who it is. You might be safer outside until they catch these criminals."

Rodney tossed his mane vigorously. "You should have told me sooner," he said. "I won't sleep outside, but I will be especially vigilant."

Charlotte shook her head. "It might be too dangerous in the barn," she said. "We can't all have someone guarding every barn every night. I don't know if a security system would do any good."

Rodney said, "No, probably not. However, since your house is so close to the barn, you are in as much danger as I am."

"You know Susie would be devastated if anything happened to you, don't you?" Charlotte said.

"I would be equally unhappy," Rodney assured her. "Thank you for the warning, and I'll take all necessary measures from now on. Please don't worry."

Charlotte still looked doubtful, and so Rodney added, "Haven't I always been right with my assessments? Don't worry. Go get some sleep."

"Okay," Charlotte said. "Susie and Jack probably won't be home until after breakfast in the school gym tomorrow morning. I remember that's how it was when I went to my first homecoming dance."

Rodney made certain physiological adjustments and increased his hearing and telepathic powers. It turned out that the two delinquents terrorizing the area were planning to set Charlotte's barn on fire that very night. They were already filling the gasoline containers to put in the trunk of the car. The fireworks were on the floor of the backseat.

Rodney went back to the trough and wolfed down a second supper. He was going to need the extra energy. Then he trotted out to the cement driveway leading from the county road to the barn, strategically depositing heaps of stool specimens at calculated intervals. It was quite satisfactory that the sky was covered with thick clouds. Moonlight or starlight might be a problem.

Then Rodney went back to his stall and waited. When he heard the evildoers about a mile away, he stood up and did the necessary breathing exercises to make himself completely invisible. Two young men drove to the farm, got out of the car quietly, opened the trunk and lifted out canisters reeking of gasoline. On the way to the barn, they both slipped in the little heaps Rodney had deposited and fell onto the concrete. Their gasoline containers broke open and spilled over the driveway. This completed step one of Rodney's plan.

He had considered impaling the both of them, but really hated the thought of having to clean his horn. So, maintaining his invisible condition, he stomped on the legs of the screaming young men while listening appreciatively to the sound of smashing bones. When he was certain they wouldn't be going anywhere, he trotted over to the farmhouse and whinnied under Charlotte's bedroom window. Charlotte turned on the lights and opened the window. "What's going on?" she asked.

Rodney whinnied impatiently until Charlotte came out the door. Then he whispered, "Charlotte, I caught your arsonists. They're lying in front of the barn. Call the sheriff. I'll go wait in my ditch behind the barn. I can't maintain this invisibility much longer."

He quickly ate a third supper on the way and then collapsed in his old ditch.

Sometime later, the sheriff's SUV drove up behind the arsonists' car, and sometime after that Rodney heard an ambulance. There was a fair amount of light and noise, but Rodney was still able to get some needed sleep.

Once everyone left, Charlotte came and found him. "The sheriff is certain they caught the arsonists," she said. "Those two had gasoline canisters and fireworks. The fireworks were the same ones they found remnants of at other barns, purchased from a dealer in Missouri who identified the two young men."

"To everyone's surprise, both of them confessed to all the barn burnings when the sheriff talked to them. Apparently something really spooked them this time."

"That sounds satisfactory," Rodney said.

"The only thing no one can explain is how the arsonists got their injuries," Charlotte continued. "They said a ghost horse tried to kill them."

"That should be obvious," Rodney said. "They slipped and fell. I had a little intestinal discomfort after supper and couldn't make it to my usual latrine area. Unfortunately I must have soiled the driveway somewhat."

"Well, yes, there is that. But two young men also had many broken bones in their legs and hoof marks on their skin," Charlotte said.

Rodney snorted. "A frightened horse might have run away when he smelled gasoline."

"But they didn't see any horses."

"Well, then they won't be setting any more barns on fire, will they?" Rodney said.

"No, and I want to thank you for that," Charlotte said. "You know, taking the law into your own hands is generally frowned upon here. In this case, however, I doubt that anyone would complain. The two young men are Mr. Morton's son and the son of the Baptist minister. The sheriff probably couldn't have done a thing without their confessions."

"Then no problem," Rodney said as he looked up. Suddenly he knew that he could leave. Susie no longer had a hold over him. And then it started raining. The driveway would soon be clean.

"I don't know what I'd do without you," Charlotte said.

Rodney looked away and felt a sense of sadness and relief at his new freedom. "You know that's not true, and you also know that it would be best if I left immediately, don't you?" he asked. "Then you can say that a horse that wandered onto your farm just wandered off again, days ago. If I'm gone, no one can sue you for damage to the young criminals because no one can prove that your horse was the hero, eh, culprit."

"Unicorns live a long, long time, much longer than a horse or a human being. Sooner or later, your neighbors would find it odd that you had such an old horse. I was no foal when I got here."

"Besides," he continued. "I've taught you enough about successful farming. You really don't need my advice anymore. Susie will miss me at first but she doesn't need me like she once did."

"You have been wanting to leave for some time now," Charlotte said. "I often see you looking off toward the horizon. Susie and I owe you so much, and we wouldn't want to force you to stay. I'll make her understand that it was time for you to leave."

"We have always understood each other's need for keeping secrets," Rodney said. "Thank you."

And he trotted off, hoping that the rain would stop soon.

THANK YOU TO OUR SUPPORTERS

Many thanks to our patrons and supporters, especially:

Wichael Tellez • carol shoemake • Bonnie Warford
Cathrin Hagey • Kate Boyes
Johanna Levene • Natalie Weizenbaum

Amy Meng • Alex grehy • Alina Kanaski • Myz Lilith
Erik DeBill • Frederick Stark • Felicia OSullivan
Salomao Becker • Anna O'Brien • Martin Cohen
J'nae Spano • Tory Hoke • S Klotz

EM Gaucher • Elana Gomel • Maria Brekke • Ana Wang •
Lorna D Keach • smokestack • Lisa Short • stolasbride
Sian Jones • Kristina Saccone • BethOfAus • J. Askew
Dirck de Lint • Wanda • K.G. Anderson
Charlotte Nash-Stewart • Suzanne Thackston • Jen G • Emily
Anderson • Maria Haskins • GriffinFire • Matthew Bennardo

Want to see your name here? Become a patron!
patreon.com/lunastation

www.ingramcontent.com/pod-product-compliance
Lightning Source LLC
Chambersburg PA
CBHW070822180626
46818CB00001B/360